The Deeds of the Ariane Novellas #3

Lark's Quest: The Choice

BARBARA COOL LEE

First Print Edition, January 2013

ISBN-13: 9781939527097

The Deeds of the Ariane Novellas

Lark's Quest:

#1: The Search
#2: The Secret
#3: The Choice

Kestrel Rising:

#4: Raven's Dilemma
#5: Lark's Exile
#6: Kestrel's Flight

Dedication

As always, for Mom, my co-writer. ☺

XI

Later that evening, Lark stood outside the door to the Lady's private rooms. After an interminable dinner with the other Ariane, where the Lady was absent and Lark was pointedly ignored by everyone except the bubbly Fawn, she had finally slipped away to come here.

There hadn't been a single hint from any other Ariane that they knew of Raven. They had all looked down their well-bred noses as Lark had repeated her story that the man she'd brought to the city was a friend of the Lady Willow's, and all had quickly accepted it as yet more evidence of the former slavegirl's inadequacy for anything but the most menial tasks. Of course, none of that was said to her directly, since she was still Number Six, and few wanted to have their swords handed to them by the slavegirl. But the message had been clear, and Lark had practically wounded herself biting her tongue to keep silent.

So now Lark could bear it no longer, and intended to discuss that anonymous friend of Willow with the Lady herself.

An elaborate embroidered portiere blocked the entrance to the Lady's quarters. It was new. It looked very fine, though the old drapery had been very pretty, too, of a pair of cranes worked in white thread on black. This one had more gold thread, and must be quite heavy, for the oak rail it hung from was obviously newer, and heavier, than before.

She thought of the people at the Black Bird Inn with their wooden cups and simple meals by the fireside. Perhaps she was beginning to understand the appeal for Lord Raven in living far away from this constant striving for more opulence. Perhaps.

She carefully pushed aside the portiere folds and stepped into the room.

The Lady Willow sat on a chair. One of her spies, the handsome one known as Wolf, was next to her. He knelt beside the chair, and his hand was in her lap.

Willow was exclaiming over his hand, which was wrapped in a white bandage.

Lark cleared her throat.

The Lady stood up abruptly, almost upsetting the man. Her reaction, more than what Lark had witnessed, made Lark uncomfortable.

Of course the Lady had spies. And this one met with her often.

But Lark had just today lectured Fawn about the folly of thinking of men, and marriage, and all that she was missing by being Ariane. It was a part of her life Lark had generally accepted without question, though lately she had found her mind turning to men—or more specifically, to one very particular man. More specific than that, parts of that one man. She felt herself blush and lowered her head. Prince Raven's hand unexpectedly clasped with hers. Prince Raven's hair falling across his forehead. Prince Raven's rare smile.

Lark didn't want to think that Willow would have one Rule for herself and another for her warriors.

She looked up again. Willow smiled at her. Lark was surprised at that smile, wistful, even sad. But perhaps she was simply ashamed at being caught in a moment of weakness.

Wolf stood up and went over to a table in the corner of the room where scrolls lay in a jumble. He kept his back to them.

"Yes, my dear?"

Lark paused, at a loss. She had wanted to catch the Lady alone to ask her about Raven, or maybe even to get permission to speak to the prince herself (for purely professional reasons, she tried to convince herself), but with that man within earshot... She looked helplessly at Willow, hoping the Lady would answer the unasked question, but Willow offered nothing.

"My Lady, is there any task—any duty—you would like me to attend to...?"

Willow frowned. "Such as?"

Such as? Lark wanted to scream, then reminded herself that she was no longer free to speak her mind. This was the way of the Ariane, keeping everything couched in polite phrases and obscure language. "I thought perhaps the matter of earlier today might not be completed, and I could offer some help in a small way...." The minor matter of the entire fate of the Silver Isle, that would be.

Willow shook her head. "It is not your concern, Lark."

Not her concern? Lark's flare of annoyance must have shown on her face, because Willow seemed to relent. "We will speak of it later. You have done a fine service, but you must trust me to handle it now."

"But, My Lady, has—has a decision been made?"

Willow sighed. "Yes, child."

Her sigh seemed to imply Raven's abdication. Lark's heart fell, but then, she surprisingly felt a surge of happiness at the thought of him returning to Rïal, with her as his escort. "Then perhaps I will need to be travelling again soon."

Willow shook her head. "No, Lark. That will not be necessary."

"Then some action will be taken here?" God, she hated these obscure conversations. "Some positive action, My Lady?"

Willow nodded. "But it will not be simple. No more questions."

My God. He had actually agreed to be king. "But, My Lady, is no one to know this?"

"Enough, Lark. I will discuss it with you later. You are becoming emotional."

God forbid she should become emotional about the king of the Silver Isle returning to his throne after a fifteen-year absence. Lark swallowed the sarcasm that threatened to erupt and tried to calm her nerves. She was Ariane. No thought, no emotion. An empty vessel in service to the king.

Willow smiled as she watched her trying to regain control. "Now, child, it seems to me you might want to leave the compound for some fresh air this evening."

Lark knew when she was being dismissed, and given how badly her hands were shaking, it was probably for the best. She bowed formally. "Thank you, My Lady."

"Would you like to take a walk, Lark?"

Lark realized with a start that this was Sabbath Eve. "Yes, My Lady. I have just returned, and do not yet have assigned duties. I thought perhaps I would take a walk into the city tonight, with your leave?" It was a ritual they observed. She pretended she was taking a walk, and Willow granted her permission, never asking where she was going.

"What about Fawn?" Willow asked. "Would you like to take her with you, on your walk?"

"Fawn? She has duty in the swordsmiths tonight." Odd that the Lady would ask. Surely she already knew that.

"I might give her leave to join you," the Lady mused. "You have spoken to Fawn since your return?" The sudden question seemed almost accusatory, and Lark felt herself bristling.

"We met in the Soft Room, My Lady," she said formally. "But we spoke only of our training."

Willow narrowed her eyes at Lark. It was a distrustful look, and Lark did not like it. "I would never betray a confidence," Lark added defensively. "My Lady, I gave my word I would not speak of—" The spy stood silently facing away from them, but she was sure he was listening to every word. "—I promised, My Lady."

Willow glanced away, breaking the stare. She walked over to the table by the spy, and glanced at one of the scrolls. "These are the latest reports?" she asked the man. He nodded.

Willow walked back over to where Lark stood. The anger, whatever had caused it, had passed. Now she looked only sad. "Forgive me, my child. I have had a bad report from the Var coast, and there is of course the other matter that is so very complicated."

"If you would prefer I stayed in, My Lady? Perhaps something will be happening...?" Surely she would be meeting with Raven again this evening, once the spy was gone. If only she would let Lark attend—Lark hated being shut out of Raven's life like this, and at such a moment in his life. "My Lady," she whispered. "Where is he?"

Willow shook her head, and glanced over her shoulder at the man. "Not now, my child. I will handle any matters that arise. Go for your walk."

Lark bowed again, then turned to go.

"Lark?"

She turned back. Willow opened her arms and Lark came forward. Once again, as she had earlier in the day, Willow kissed her on the forehead. But this time it felt like a farewell. "You have done well."

Without another word, Willow turned away, dismissing her.

Lark turned and left the chamber.

Raven opened his eye, but saw nothing, and fear washed over him. Was he completely blind now? He stilled the panic that beat in his chest and tried to think.

As his vision slowly adjusted to the darkness he realized he was not blinded—any more than he had been before.

His one good eye still saw. Some soft diffused light made outlines faintly visible in the black room. And a dozen paces from where he lay on the floor, a crack of light was barely visible.

More than a crack. It was a faint rectangle on the wall. A door. It was the light shining around the edges of a well-fitted door.

Raven tried to sit up, but fell back. His head ached, and he felt a stickiness on the back of his neck. He reached one hand back. He winced as his hand met the cut, blood still sluggishly oozing from it. He had been hit by someone, and now he was here. He tried to remember.

The floor was hard and cool. He lay against its smoothness for a while longer, gathering his strength, and his courage, to try again.

He heard some faint tapping far away. The sound tickled the edge of his mind, and he tried to make sense of it through his fogged consciousness. He had heard that sound before. Where? The tapping was so familiar, like some common background noise remembered from his childhood. That thought was followed by horror, as he realized he must be somewhere near his childhood home—the last place in the world he wanted to be.

Driven by the fear, he again tried to sit up, more successfully this time. Though he could not manage to make it fully to a sitting position, he was able to lean against his elbows and rest there, his head above the surface of the floor.

It felt like a victory of sorts.

The tapping continued. Very far away, like listening to the thud of horses galloping across a plain in the distance. Rhythmic, a well-trained pattern of blows against—

He remembered. It was the sound of the Ariane mines where the rare silvery metal was forged into magical swords.

Far below ground the smiths worked, in shops reached only by secret tunnels. He was in the catacombs? The catacombs led to the underground workshops of the Arianesmiths. The secret passageways were known only to royals... and the Ariane who served them.

He had been in the royal tombs. He did remember that. And the royal tombs held a door leading into the tunnel system. So it was possible someone had brought him into the tunnels. But now where was he? That door he could see in the wall made no sense. There were no doors like that one in the tunnels under the Funerary Hill. From where he lay he could see the door was clearly not one of the secret entrances the ancient builders had fitted into the tunnels, nor could it be the heavy carved door that blocked his mother's tomb, God forbid. He was not in the tombs.

But it all felt vaguely familiar.

He turned his head, and realized that on his blind side the answer had been there all along.

High up on the wall was a window, with moonlight shining faintly through. Placed at a height of five men from the floor, the window was round, about the diameter of a man's waist. And it was barred, with heavy iron bars fanning out from its center like a spider's web.

Raven lay back against the floor in defeat. He now knew exactly where he was. The only place in the world where windows too high for any normal person to reach needed such bars.

The Ariane prison.

Lark ducked under a low bridge as she walked beside one of the main canals. Straight down she had come from the Mission into the city of Chÿar, not that long a walk but a world away. She was now on the floor of the cauldron at the center of Chÿar mountain. The floor would be underwater if not for the interlaced canals that channeled the water between banks of raised soil. Control the water, and you control the city. The canals were the central feature of the city, an unpleasant but necessary part of the fabric of city life. The nobles lived in houses up on the hillsides, above the stink of the canals and the crowded, dangerous paved streets.

The peasants and workers lived down on the flat of the city floor, surrounded by the dank canal stench and living in constant fear of a break in the levees that held the water in control. As she walked, she could hear the canal water sloshing against the levees with a suck of water against slime-clad stone.

The streets were dark. The black stone of the paving reflected little moonlight. She also reflected little light. She wore her Ariane cloak inside out, muffling the glitter of silver mesh and showing only the padded silk lining. All in ghostly pale gray, she walked unseen in the streets, near-invisible to casual passers-by. It was best to be unnoticed. The people of the city would shrink in fear if they saw an Ariane in their midst. And where she was going, it was best not to be noticed. She was about to commit treason.

All around her the main streets were paved in ornate mosaic

patterns—moths and swans, flowers and Ma trees, alabaster deer and obsidian griffons. The moonlight illuminated the figures (the same moon Raven might be looking at this evening, she mused, but then, yet again, tried to let the thought of him go). The mosaics were cracked and filthy, like the city itself. The large buildings of stone were magnificently crafted, but now gone to squalor as no one worked to maintain them.

On the canal beside her as she walked she could see a woman and young child in a small boat. They worked by the light of a lantern hung from the stern, dipping baskets over the side into the canal water and bringing them up, picking out the contents, and then repeating the movement. Snails for supper. They would eat better than many tonight.

She left the path along the canalside and turned into a familiar street. A group of peasants were coming down the narrow street toward her, but when they caught sight of the Ariane they quickly scattered into doorways and down alleys. She had grown used to being accepted as an equal while pretending to be a peasant on her travels, and now she was back here with a silver wall between her and the people, keeping them apart. She sighed, and kept going.

The fog from the canals drifted into the street where the poor huddled around their straw fires. The smoke burned the lungs, and away from the canals, the buildings crowded close, leaning over her head, stacked up until no patch of moonlight made it down to street level.

Again she made a turn in the darkness, passing the Spinners House, the Weavers House, and the Dyers House, all lined up like brick tombs along the street. Every step of the production of silk was prescribed by law. First the peasants in the outlying villages grew the cocoons. They sold them at market, paying a tax to the local ruling family and to the Ariane representatives of the Griffons. Then the cocoons were brought to Chÿar, where they were sold to spinners, who paid the double tax again. Then the spinners sold to the weavers, who paid double tax, and then to the dyers, who paid double tax. No wonder there were smugglers. How else would anyone make enough to live on, after taxes? The silk was unique in all the known world, and should be valuable enough to bring wealth to everyone, but it never seemed to work out that way.

Lark turned down an alley, then stopped at a door no more or less decrepit than the rest, and knocked.

Silence inside. She rapped on the door again, her gray doeskin glove picking up a stain from the moldy wood.

The door cracked open. It was a woman Lark didn't recognize.

"Ariane?" The word was an entreaty. "This is the wrong house."

Lark smiled, looking as non-threatening as was possible for a fully garbed Ariane in a Chÿar alley on a dark night. "I am here to see Spinner."

The woman looked more terrified. "He is innocent."

How to explain herself to this stranger? It was hard enough to explain to herself what she was doing here. She was here to commit a crime. Lark stood there, at a loss.

The door swung wide. A man with few teeth, little hair, but a big grin stood there.

"Well, well. Come in, Sister."

He hugged her close, and she embraced him back. "Thank you for the welcome, Spinner. I am sorry. I did not have time to change."

"No worry, no worry. It is a pleasure to see you after so long. Come inside." She went in.

The room looked like any other poor hut, a pile of straw in the corner, ready to burn for heat.

She handed Spinner the bag she had carried down from the Mission. The bundle of cocoons Raven had bought in Sÿun would be worth much to this family, and she had cached a bottle of wine as well.

"This is a great gift. The other one also brought gifts, but your presence has been missed." It was traditional not to mention the names of other worshippers for safety reasons, but she knew Spinner was proud to tell her that Fawn had been coming on her own.

Spinner and the woman shifted the straw to reveal the trap door beneath.

"Come, come in. You are most welcome here."

The cave beneath the hut was dank and cold, and dripped from the seepage of the canal one street over. But the tiny cellar was filled with smiling faces. A larger crowd than she'd seen, more than a dozen in total, gathered here, whispering among themselves.

They fell silent at her entrance. She recognized a few faces, but most were not familiar, and they looked at her—or more accurately, at her garb—with suspicion.

"Welcome our Sister, my friends. She is an old friend, but has been absent for many services."

He motioned for her to sit. Spinner called her Sister, as she was called Sister by the Ariane. She had tried to parse the distinction between the two sisterhoods before, but gave up and simply accepted the term.

"I apologize," she said to them all. "I do not usually come dressed so. It is not appropriate in this place."

"All are welcome who come in peace, Lark. No one must apologize for who or what he is in this room. Please—" he motioned to the small table, set with a small loaf and a knife.

She bowed, touched that he honored her so. His son, called Spinner also, handed her the knife.

She saw how the skin on his hand was newly scarred-over, the burn so deep that the boy's fingers curled into the palm. She touched his hand gently. It was the silk-spinners' mark, and he was only ten years old.

"The water was hot that day," the boy whispered.

"I understand." The silk cocoons must be soaked in near-boiling water until the translucent strands unwound and were picked out of the water by nimble fingers. It took quick, expert work to pull the individual filaments and spin them together into usable threads of fine silk. If one was in a hurry to make a quota, it was easy to get burned.

His father clapped the boy roughly on the shoulder, with a scarred hand just like his son's. "It would happen sometime. The water is hot, and one has work to do." He said it gruffly. "It's nothing to fret about. Never bothered me none." But he turned away quickly and bowed his head so Lark couldn't see his face.

The people around nodded. They all understood. Thin and hungry and smelly, they worked until their quotas were met, bathed in the canal when they could, and then drank the water from the same canal and grew ill and died young, or became twisted and shrunken with palsy and coughs that never left. Could Raven really fix this? Would he?

Lark bowed to them silently in respect, then took the knife and cut the triangle in the bread offering. All joined in a prayer of thanks for their many blessings, then she cut the bread into small pieces so all could have a bite.

XII

Lark was reading aloud from the tattered pages of a partial Book, the most complete one they had found. The words were taken in by this small group like a treasure.

Suddenly they heard a footstep in the room above their heads.

Lark paused.

"Is someone on guard above?" she said softly to Spinner.

He shook his head.

Lark closed the book and handed it to Spinner the younger. He removed a brick from the wall and put the book in the niche, then replaced the brick.

The group muttered and stirred. "Silence!" Lark whispered.

She motioned them toward the back of the little cave.

Spinner the Elder lifted a second trap door slowly, and peeked out. He ducked his head back down and nodded to the group.

Lark took the rear, herding them toward the escape route and hushing them when they made any sound.

She was the last one out. After a look to see that the candle was doused and the traces of bread and wine had been hidden away, she climbed up into the room.

Lark was in a tiny shed, redolent with chicken droppings and straw. She quickly closed the trapdoor and used her boot to scatter the straw to cover the opening. The shed had no door, and faced out onto a different alley than the one by which she had entered.

The shed was completely empty.

She peeked out the door. Nothing. Where had everyone gone?

"This way," someone whispered. It was the boy. He was just beyond the door, in a shadow created by the overhanging roof. He reached out his scarred hand to her. She took it.

"They have taken the others," he whispered. He pointed back to the left.

She led him to the right, and they exited the alley to find themselves on the main canal path.

A hundred paces away she saw a sight that broke her heart.

All her fellow worshippers, including Spinner the Elder, were in a small group surrounded by Ariane guards.

Lark paused in the alleyway, unsure what to do.

Spinner the elder glanced her way. He was being shackled by the guard, and Lark started forward.

He shook his head. She stopped.

The Ariane shackling him noticed he was staring into the dark alley, and, with a quick word to another guard, came toward Lark and the boy, who ducked back in the shadow of the buildings. Lark was too far away in the dimness to recognize the Ariane's face, but she knew if she was found it would be disaster.

Suddenly, Spinner the Younger gave her hand a quick squeeze, let go of it, and stepped out of the alley in front of the guard. "Why are you arresting my father?" he said with an impressive show of bravado.

The guard—it was Feather, one of Lotus's cronies—grabbed the boy without a word and dragged him back to the group.

Lark stood helplessly watching the peasants being chained together, then quickly turned her back, and ran down the canal path in the opposite direction.

Lark burst through the door of Willow's private chamber without ceremony.

Though it had been hours since she left, the spy called Wolf was still there with the Lady, and now Lotus was there, too.

Lotus turned to Lark with a frown, but the other two continued their whispered conversation over the scrolls on the table in the far corner.

Lark waited, impatient. She had run all the way back to the Mission, ready to confront Willow about the capture of her friends, and now....

Lark bowed to Willow. "My Lady, may I speak to you?" It was difficult to restrain her impatience.

Willow looked up coldly. "Your hair is mussed, Lark. You should not appear before me so disheveled."

Lark nodded, swallowing the sharp retort that sprang to mind. "Yes, My Lady." She ran a hand through her hair, trying to smooth it.

She glanced at Lotus, expecting some smirk at seeing Lark chastised. Lotus's expression was a cold echo of Willow's, unreadable.

Lark tapped her foot on the floor. What was going on here? The Lady knew she went to the city. Surely the Lady herself would have told her not to go to the meeting if something was planned. Why, she had even encouraged her to take Fawn along.

Finally, Willow turned and nodded curtly to Lotus and Wolf. "Leave us."

They left the room, Wolf without so much as a word, but as Lotus went out she glanced back at Lark with a very unhappy look.

If Lotus was unhappy, it could only be good news for Lark. So what was going on?

Lark paced the floor.

Willow stood by the table, arms folded. "You have something to say, Lark?"

Now that she was here, Lark was not certain how to bring up the subject. It was not Lark's place to question the Lady's decisions. But how could the Lady have called for a raid on the peasants when she knew Lark was in the city? Or had she known?

She looked at Willow, trying to decide how to proceed. She

flopped into a chair, at a loss.

Willow finally spoke, calmly, coldly, with the air of majesty Lark had seen many times, but which she rarely used when alone with Lark. "Stand when I speak to you, Lark."

Lark stood up. "My Lady, I was in the city tonight."

"Yes, I know."

"Then you know what happened."

Willow's look was unreadable. "I know you have disappointed me."

"Disappointed you? My Lady, you have always known—"

"—That you persist in following the peasant superstition? I have hoped you would outgrow this—this remnant of your slave background."

Lark forced herself to unclench her fists. "You ordered a raid on my friends, My Lady."

"Your friends are your fellow Ariane here in the Mission, Lark. Don't ever forget that."

"My friends? They have never accepted me! I am always Lark the Slave to them!"

Willow stopped her with a look. "If this is how you behave, then I am not surprised, Lark. An Ariane is not so emotional. Your behavior is menial. Compose yourself."

The Lady Willow went to the table in the corner and poured herself a goblet of sweet wine. She stood there and sipped it, her back to Lark.

Lark waited, fuming. She would not win a battle of wills with the Lady. She must find a way to reason with her. "My Lady, please. My friends... the peasants arrested tonight. They are innocent."

"Of meeting secretly to talk of peasant treason?"

"They met to worship, yes. But My Lady. Shouldn't Raven be the one to decide if it is treason?"

"Raven? You speak of him with such disrespect and expect me to believe you are not corrupted by these peasants?"

"He was called by that name during his hiding, My Lady. I meant no disrespect. But shouldn't His Grace have something to say about this?"

"You are questioning my judgment?"

"No, My Lady," Lark said carefully, shifting her weight from one foot to the other. "But, His Grace...?"

"Will be consulted about this matter in the morning. He is... resting now. Now stop fidgeting. It is unbecoming of your rank."

"He will not approve," Lark said with certainty. "You know he will not."

"The guards were perhaps overzealous," Willow acknowledged.

"But the people they arrested—"

"The peasants?" Willow shook her head. "They are nothing."

"Rav—the prince will not think so." That was an understatement. She would like to be a witness in the morning when Willow found herself on the receiving end of Raven's withering contempt.

"Perhaps."

"Where are they? What are you going to do with them?"

"They will get a bit of a scare and then be sent home. Now stop worrying about it." A wave of her hand dismissed the peasants. "You're not wearing the pearls, Lark?"

Lark pulled them out from the neckline of her tunic. "My Lady—" she said helplessly.

"You should show them. They are precious, you know. I have shown you great honor, Lark. You should appreciate it."

"I do appreciate it, My Lady. I appreciate everything you have done for me. But—"

Willow walked away from her, back to the table littered with scrolls. "Come here, Lark. I have had disturbing news."

"Yes, My Lady," Lark said slowly.

"Var pirates are heading to the coast. They will be here in three days. My spy has just brought me a report." She always called him her spy, though Lark was sure he was much more than that.

Lark tried to reorganize her thoughts. How did this relate to what happened in the city?

Willow stood silently, expecting some response.

"Yes, My Lady," Lark said again.

"My spy was injured by the Var, but escaped with his life to bring the news."

Lark doubted the story. The man always looked like he'd just come from some woman's bedchamber, not from a battle, but this was not as important as her friends.

"Come here, child."

Lark came to stand beside her.

"A troop of our best soldiers, and a hundred peasant conscripts are here." She pointed to something on the scroll in front of her.

The map was of the Var Shore. Lark put aside everything else and concentrated while Willow told her about the noble soldier who led the troop of archers, and the usual plan for deployment of troops.

"Do you understand?"

"Yes, My Lady," she finally said. "But—"

"I am sending my ten best Ariane to this battle. The Var must not win this time. You will do whatever it takes to drive them back. Do you understand?"

"Yes, My Lady."

"Lark—" There was suddenly a catch in Willow's voice, and she hugged Lark close. "It is your first command. It is a reward for your great service to me. I expect you to win this for me. And for the King."

It was a great honor, and completely unexpected. "But I have never—I mean, Lotus has always—"

"—Lotus understands her place. You will lead this battle." Willow handed her the map, then turned away, dismissing her with a nod.

"Yes, My Lady." Lark paused. "But, My Lady, in the city tonight —"

"We will talk of it after the battle."

"—But the people captured?"

"—The traitors detained, you mean?"

Lark nodded, painfully. "Yes, My Lady. I wish to—"

"—We will speak of it later. You must ride for the coast tonight. You are dismissed."

Lark started to go, then turned back. "But, My Lady—"

"Obedience was never your strong point, Lark. What is it?"

"The prince? My friends? What is happening?"

Willow looked down at the table. "Great changes are afoot. Play your part and—" She choked something back. "—trust me as you always have, my child."

Lark bowed and left the room.

When Raven awoke after more blessed unconsciousness his prison was visible at least, which was some small improvement. In the light of day he could see he had been right. He was in the royal prison beneath the Ariane Mission. Once he was knocked out someone must have carried or dragged him through the secret passageways from the royal tombs all the way to here.

He looked at his clothes, torn and ragged. Dragged, from the looks of it.

The back of his neck was bruised where he had been hit. He remembered that now. The mocking voice, then the blows from behind. The voice had been male. He was sure of that. But he was in a prison guarded by women warriors. This did not make any sense.

Not only were the Ariane women, they were his guards, damn it. He felt outrage that he was being treated so by his own servants. It had been a long time since he had thought of them so, but it was a fact.

He stood up, bracing himself against the smooth obsidian wall. His hand slipped, and he fell again, wrenching his damned knee.

He stifled a curse and tried again. The walls were glass-smooth, and it was hard to get a purchase on them. Finally he stood, and limped over to the door. Heavy iron hinges and a sturdy lock. Not much chance at breaking through there. He had best settle in for a long stay.

And it would be long, from the looks of it. Raising a hand against him would be the way to eternal damnation for any true believer in the nobles' gods. The Ariane would have to keep him alive here, for they could not harm him. Or could they? What if everything Lark had told him had been a lie?

Lark had been a slave. That in itself never made any sense. No slave had ever become an Ariane. Maybe everything she had said, everything she claimed to be was an illusion. If she was not really Ariane, then she was not bound by their code of honor. But that skill she had shown in the forest, her very bearing, every feeling he had toward her, told him she spoke the truth. No one could pretend to be Ariane. The garb, the sword, and more than that, the skill and quicker-than-light movement—it was not something a person masqueraded.

But Lark had been a peasant first. What if she did not believe in the nobles' gods? Ultimately, it was only faith that kept order in the Silver Isle. If peasants did not believe the royal family's right to rule came from the gods, they could—and history proved they would—burn them alive. If Lark did not believe her power came from the noble gods, she could throw him in prison, and somehow trick the other Ariane into going along with her plot, whatever it was.

The implications were chilling.

He tried to remember the words from the Book of the Dead. He whispered in the cell, his voice echoing around the walls: "Anoint my body in sweet unguents, and wrap me in fine cloths so my body may be preserved for all time. Oh Gatekeeper, receive my body into the ship of the dead, with my beloved King as pilot and guide. Place the sacred herbs in my mouth so I be reunited in body and soul, my bones healed of all weakness, my spirit anewed in my flesh, so that I may live eternally as I have in life, in the role you have ordained for me, by my King's grace and for his service."

For my king's service. And if one believed otherwise? Then did he, Raven yr Griffon, last of the line of kings and only living heir to the Scepter of the Silver Isle, serve any purpose? Or was it better that he was gone from the world, so his people could get on with the business of living their lives without him?

No. Raven thought of Old Ox, and Mouse, and of the silk-smuggling stableman and his sickly child, and of the noble woman so fearful of the Ariane that she trembled at their coming. And he thought of the hunger in the streets and the execution of peasant worshippers. No. His life was worthless, but theirs were not. Someone must speak for the people. Someone must stand up to this. And unfortunately, as crippled and foolish and completely incompetent as he was, it appeared that that someone would have to be him.

He scouted around on the floor until he found a small stone. He propped himself up against the smooth wall by the door and began to tap at the iron nail holding one of the hinges in place. It did not move, but he had time. He had his entire life, it appeared. He kept tapping at the nail. There was more at stake here than his own miserable life, and it was time he did something about it.

XIII

They traveled swiftly, ten Ariane on the best horses in the land. It took them only two days to reach the coast.

There was little talk. At least, there was little talking directed toward Lark. The others resented her leadership, that was clear enough. They spoke among themselves in low tones, but seldom acknowledged her presence unless directly addressed. Lotus in particular seemed preoccupied, lost in thoughts Lark didn't want to imagine.

Only Fawn seemed cheerful. This was to be her first battle, and she bubbled with excitement as they approached the southern coastline. It was her first time out of Chÿar since she was five, as it turned out, and she was all atwitter with the thrill of seeing the countryside. Her chatter was a welcome break from the uncomfortable silences of the others, though Lark was concerned about what lay ahead, particularly for Fawn in her limited skill. Why had Willow insisted on sending Fawn along? Perhaps she felt Lark needed a friend beside her. She certainly had no one else to trust. The image of Raven flashed through her mind, but she dismissed it. Thinking of the crown prince as a friend, or worse, as a man, was sheer foolishness. She was his servant, and the closeness she had felt from him on the journey was just the heightened emotion that came from being close to such a man as he.

She looked up to see Lotus glowering at her, and briefly wished that the Lady—and Raven himself—had not made her promise to keep his return such a secret. It would give them courage in the coming battle. And she had to admit to herself, it would also give her some much-needed respect from the other Ariane if she could tell them she had done what she swore to do all those years ago.

She noticed that Fawn was suddenly very still as she rode beside her.

They had just passed the top of a coastal hill, and as Lark looked up she saw the remains of the outpost that had been destroyed in the last Var raids.

Everything was gone. The ground itself was black with soot, and the stonework was licked with streaks of charring. The horse's hooves kicked up the ash that coated the ground, making a cloud that choked them all.

A gleam of white showed where a soldier had fallen at his post, burned to bone.

Fawn's eyes were wide, and Lark could not think of how to comfort her.

Why had Willow chosen her for this task? If this was the reward for returning the prince, she would have preferred another useless bit of jewelry like the pearl necklace. She had never been good at leading others. That was why her searches for Raven had been such a welcome respite from her other duties. To be alone, away from the politics and shifting currents of power in the Ariane world, had been a gift. Now it was gone forever, and she was left with the "honor" of leading warriors who did not trust her.

She shouldn't worry about it. The battle would be fought on the traditional plan, as they all had been trained to fight. She had no real decisions to make, except how to somehow keep everyone in order when her own people would not listen to her.

What had Willow said? She had done a lifetime's work in finding Raven, and nothing would ever be the same. She should remember that. When she returned from battle he would be ready to ascend the throne, and she would witness something worthy of memorializing in legend forever. She was sure that Raven could save the Silver Isle from ruin, and she could take satisfaction in having been a small part of making it happen.

When Raven was king, he would set things right. He would free the peasant worshippers, reduce the taxes, who knows what all he would do. But for now she must do as Willow said. Trust in her leader, and attend to the task at hand.

The path rounded a curve in the hill, and suddenly the sea was spread below them. They halted and scanned the horizon. The sky was leaden gray, and the sea was dark gray, streaked with white waves where the wind churned the water. Not a single sail could be seen. They still had time.

"Look!" Fawn said. She pointed excitedly to the ruins on the shore, where smoke rose from the peasant camp and the bright silk pennants whipped in the wind over the noble archers' tents.

With a sigh, Lark urged her mount forward. She had a battle to win.

The fog had rolled in on the coast, and soon the Var ships would come streaking out of it to attack them on the shore.

Lark strode toward the meeting tent set up on the shingle above the high tide line. Her cloak shimmered in her wake as she walked. All around her the fog swirled like smoke. Whale's breath, Raven's father had called it. When she was little she had thought he had meant it literally, her imagination conjuring great ocean beasts exhaling plumes of smoke out on the sea.

Real monsters lurked on this sea. The Var ships had been spotted on the horizon by the local fisherfolk. These foreign warriors had won again and again. They lurked offshore, then struck at dawn, overwhelming the natives with their superior brute force and wild, savage fighting style.

To stop the Var they must do something different this time, something decisive. Why had the Lady Willow thought that she could win this battle? The local peasants huddled outside the tent, waiting for orders, waiting for help from the nobles within. She must figure out some way not to lose this battle, for lives were at stake.

The peasant crowd parted to let her through. She pushed aside the tent flap and stepped inside.

A tall man with an arrogant carriage bowed to her, sweeping aside his crimson velvet cloak. "Reed yr Täryn," he said. She nodded to him. Täryn was on the coast near the Black Spines. He had traveled far to get here. "I have fifty archers. A hundred more are coming, but will not arrive in time. It is only my fifty and your ten against twenty Var ships."

"Along with a hundred peasants," Lark corrected.

He looked startled. "They do not count, of course, My Lady Ariane."

"Everyone counts," Lark corrected him. The long bow he carried was clearly worn from much use. She must find a way to win his trust.

She turned to Fawn, who stared at Reed with a look of wonder. He did not seem to notice. "Fawn, bring me the leader of the peasants."

Fawn took her eyes from the man, turned, and left the tent.

Reed stared after her. "Her name is Fawn?" he asked.

Lark nodded, distracted. "We must do something different, Reed yr Täryn."

He was not listening. He turned away and watched the door until Fawn reappeared.

Fawn returned with a young man in rags. The man scurried behind the Ariane, looking very thin and ragged in comparison to the sleek Ariane and nobles now surrounding him.

As the man approached, Reed stepped back, pulling his cloak away so it did not touch the man.

"Your name?" Lark asked the peasant.

"River," he whispered.

She turned to the archer. "Why do you shrink from touching him, Täryn?"

He answered as if she were stupid. "We do not touch their kind."

"Why?" Lark persisted.

He looked confused. "It has always been so."

Lark was beginning to get an idea. "I see. And you do things because you have always done them."

"And my fathers before me."

"I see. That is a good reason. Did your fathers before you have a cure for the Var scourge?"

"Of course not," he looked a bit annoyed, but took her catechism without complaint. "If we had a cure, we would not be here, Lady."

"Yet you are here."

"We have always come in times of need."

She nodded. She looked at the peasant. "As have this man's forefathers."

Reed bristled at that, but then, after a pause, nodded. "We all have our place in the Silver Isle."

"Yes. But it is not enough, is it?"

"Lady?"

"We come, all of us—" the sweep of her hand took in all gathered in the room as well as the peasants gathered out in the fog —"and we fight the Var, and we lose, and we are pushed back, and our villages are sacked."

She heard a murmur go through the crowd in the tent, and an echo of fear in the peasants outside.

"An inspirational speech, Sister." Lotus's voice was scornful. "Shall we gather around the fire and sing songs of brotherhood now?"

Lark shook her head. "Of course not. That is not the way of the people of the Silver Isle, is it?" She raised her voice slightly, talking over the frightened murmurs in the back. "So we do what we always do. We wait until the Var come to us. We send the untrained peasants out in front on the shoreline, on foot with their poor weapons and little skill, because their lives are less valuable. The noble archers can stand back on this hill and take aim at the Var as they come ashore. And the Ariane can strike last, after the peasants have gone in and been defeated. And we will make our ancestors proud that we did things just as they have always done."

She was losing them. They talked openly now of leaving, or hiding. Reed raised his hand to the archers, and they fell silent. The Ariane silently watched Lark.

Reed did not smile, but he looked at her expectantly. "Or?" he said simply.

She thought of Prince Raven's long-ago Martyrsday speech. *We are of one flesh, father. All of us.*

She nodded to Reed. "Or we will do something we have never done before. We will work together."

Lotus scoffed. "It is not done." She waved a hand at the peasant, who looked as if he wanted to run, but did not dare to. "These are not trainable. Would you have them stand back and watch us fight? Would you have us take the brunt of the attack to save your kind?" There was more muttering from the crowd. Surely they had all noticed Lark was not a noble, and yet she was leading these Ariane. They began to say as much, wondering what right she had to order them around. "It is not done that way, Lark," Lotus said again, and all around her nodded in agreement.

Lark nodded to her as well. "That is so. We follow the rules we learned from our forefathers. We will hold to our traditions, and we will not change, and when we lie stiffening in our graves we can take pride in our steadfast allegiance to our time-honored traditions. *We never changed in response to new ways,* our gravestones will read." She turned back to the archers. "But before the Var reach shore you may wish to send word to your family of your burial preferences."

Silence again, this time so long Lark was sure she'd lost them.

Reed finally smiled. "You speak the truth, and do it well enough, My Lady. I do not wish to lose more brothers." He turned and bowed toward Lark and to Fawn standing beside her. "Or sisters. I will fight beside a dog if he fights against the Var."

The other nobles muttered among themselves, but Reed's opinion clearly carried weight. He ignored the men's mutterings and spoke directly to Lark. "I will follow you, Lady Ariane. What is your plan?"

Lark smiled. "If you want to hunt a whale, you do not sit on the shore. You go out where the whales are."

Mouse watched Old Oxen cast about the mountainside. He was quietly searching for something.

"What are you looking for?" Mouse asked.

"Shhh. Sound carries on this mountain."

The mountain that held the city of Chÿar seemed to be nothing but bare slopes of rain-slick, impassible rock. He and Ox had been scrambling up these bare rocks for the whole day, it seemed to Mouse. There was a road to their left, but Oxen had steered them away from it, instead insisting on this tortuous path. Mouse understood. They were on a secret mission. They didn't want the guards at the city's entrance to find them. But since they were still heading toward the top of the mountain, and the top of the mountain held a mean-looking guard tower manned by undoubtedly mean-looking guards, he didn't understand what Oxen planned to do.

Mouse had always wanted to see Chÿar. He, like everyone in the countryside, had heard it was a glorious city, full of gleaming paved streets and flowing waters and rich hillsides of rich, growing grains. The tax collectors who came periodically from the city were always dressed in fine clothes and rode sleek, beautiful horses. Any city they came from must be magnificent. But from what he had seen of the barren mountain topped by a crown of thick fog, it seemed the stories of Chÿar were false.

Mouse crept up behind Oxen, who seemed to be lost, looking under rocks and behind bushes for something. "Where's the city?" he asked again, as he had earlier.

"Hush." Oxen dragged Mouse over behind a scrubby bush and knelt down in front of him. "The city is on the inside," he whispered, "like a cauldron scooped out of the center of the mountain by a great hand."

"I want to see it," Mouse whispered. "If that's where Master Raven is, then we should go there."

"If you don't shut up, it'll be the last thing you do see. Now be patient and stop bothering me."

Oxen made for a small fold in the mountainside, where feeble scrub jutted out from the tumble of rocks.

Mouse picked his way through the rock. "Careful," whispered Ox. "Start a landslide and the soldiers'll be on us for sure."

Mouse tried to tread carefully so he didn't set anything sliding. The way was steep, and the rocks seemed barely stable—breathing on them might send them tumbling down the mountainside.

Periodically Mouse stopped, hesitating, trying to find a path. At those moments Oxen sometimes picked him up bodily and lifted him over a seemingly impossible spot, then set him down in some place even more unsteady.

Above them piles of bare rock still stood, mocking them. Where could this possibly lead? Oxen had a plan, but Mouse couldn't see what it was.

The part of the mountain still above them was obviously too steep to climb. Unless there was another way in, this was a dead end. They would have to go back to the road.

Finally they made their way into a small gully, a fold in the mountainside that temporarily hid them from the gate tower above. The tower was not so far above them now. They had climbed nearly to the top.

"Stay here." Ox scouted around, apparently looking for the key he had insisted would be on the mountain.

Mouse scrambled over to Ox. "I can help look." Ox had said something about a key that was supposed to be here. Mouse didn't see how there could be a key hidden among the scrub on the mountain, and he didn't see what the key would unlock anyway, but Ox was getting angry at him asking so many questions, so Mouse just kept looking on the ground for something that looked important.

Mouse trod on a pile of branches and the ground gave way

under him. He felt himself fall, and made what he would have sworn was only a small yelp of surprise, but Oxen was at his side in an instant, grabbing his arm and hauling him upright.

"Silence! Unless you want the guards to find you."

"Did the guards see?" Mouse shaded his eyes and tried to spot the figures in the gate tower.

Oxen pulled him back under the cover of a shrub. The shrub had thorns, and Mouse tried to twist away.

"Hold still. If the guards find us, that's the end of it."

"Are they Ariane?"

"No. They're duty soldiers—sons of noblemen doing their service. Spoiled brats, mostly, spoiled by their families and now armed and armored and spoiling to put their shiny new swords to use. We don't want to meet any of them." Ox had been saying things like that lately, stuff about how the people in the city lived, and what the soldiers did, and things that made Mouse think Ox knew more about the city than Mouse had ever realized before.

"But how will we get in to see Master Raven?"

"If he's still alive," Oxen muttered. "He must be. Lark wouldn't kill him outright. She'd bring him back to the ruling witch." Oxen noticed him staring and stopped. "Come on. We're wasting time here. We've a long way to go."

"To the secret entrance?"

"It's not exactly an entrance."

"What is it?"

"An exit." Mouse must have looked confused, because Oxen said, "I'm looking for a hole in the ground, boy."

"Is that all? I found one." Mouse pointed to where the ground had given way under the brush, a few yards from the bush where they crouched.

Ox motioned for him to stay put, then made his way quietly over to the spot. He pulled aside the brush, and then motioned for Mouse to come closer.

With the brush cleared away Mouse could see that the hole was smooth—clearly man-made. It was sided with black stone as far down as he could see, which wasn't more than a man's height down. The hole seemed to go on to some unknown depth, and some smell wafted up, dank and stale. The hole made his skin crawl.

"What is it?"

"A burial shaft," Ox said shortly. "The king's spirit needs an exit to walk the world each day."

"So it floats up out of there?"

"Something like that."

Mouse knew the nobles' religion said stuff like that. The bodies of rich people were carefully preserved in tombs in the city, and the slaves and peasants were buried near them to serve them in the afterlife. It didn't make any sense. The peasants' God said the body was just a shell that held the soul; the nobles' god said the body must be preserved so one could perform the same duties after death as in life. Slaves remained slaves for eternity, kings remained kings. It was all too complicated to understand. But Mouse thought maybe it was important information for saving Master Raven, so he tried to figure it out.

"Why isn't it guarded?" he whispered

"Because there's no way out of there alive."

Mouse digested that for a moment. "If we die, then how can we save Master Raven?"

"If your master is dead, we are dead. If there is no key, if the shaft has been blocked at the bottom, if the door is barred, if it's too late to save him anyway, we will die. Do you want to run home now?"

Mouse set his jaw. "He needs us. Let's go get him out of the hole."

Oxen gave him as close to a smile as he'd ever seen on the old man. Ox lifted him up by his armpits and just before letting him go said, "Don't scream."

He dropped Mouse down the hole.

XIV

The coracle rocked under the weight of one Ariane warrior, two archers, and two peasant rowers. The small boat was not made to brave the sea outside the bay with such weight aboard, but they were going to try it.

The boats were loaded quietly, each with their mixed load of fighters, and began to shove off from the shingle, one by one heading into the fog.

No one spoke, on Lark's order. The boat oars were wrapped in cloth to muffle their creaking against the oarlocks.

Was this error?

She didn't know. She could not understand why the Lady Willow had given her this charge. She felt so unprepared to have all these lives at her command. The thought struck her that this was what Raven had worried about—that any wrong decision on his part meant many people would die. She suddenly realized she had judged him too harshly.

Fawn looked over at her, eyes wide with fear. Without speaking, Lark gave her a look meant to convey encouragement and confidence. Lark had wanted to leave her on shore, but Lotus insisted that she could not be spared, and must pull her share like the other Ariane.

Lark went closer to Fawn. Her boat was almost ready. "I am

afraid, Lark," she whispered.

Lark hadn't the heart to hush her. Instead, she took her hand. It trembled. Fawn could not fight like this. With a sigh, Lark touched Fawn's shoulder, and made the connection. Fawn's eyes widened as she felt the surge of confidence from Lark. "You cannot," she whispered. "It will weaken you."

Lark shook her head. "Remember everything you have learned —you can do it," she whispered to Fawn. She helped her into the boat, then turned away.

Her own boat was last to launch. Reed yr Täryn, another archer called Flame, and four peasants, including River and his cousin, joined her in the leaky craft.

They set off. They heard nothing but the sounds of the sea around them—water, gulls and wind. Lark could feel the damp cold through her cloak, and she hugged it closer around her. The faint jingling of the mesh seemed loud in the boat. All eyes turned to her, and she tried to look confident for them.

They could see nothing but the gray fog shrouding them, and the gray sea waiting to swallow them up if they made any mistake.

The Var ships were hidden by the fog, but their crew would also be unable to see. She was betting that this surprise would even the odds. She was betting all their lives on it.

They all tried to breathe quietly and listen. Yes, there was the creak of wood to the left. Lark motioned to the rowers to head that way.

There it was. A dark shape loomed ahead. "We must not waste our arrows," she whispered to Reed. He nodded.

Closer, closer. The dark hull was there. The Var ship was anchored, and rode heavy in the water. The Var were waiting for daylight, as they always did. The ship was quiet.

Lark realized in alarm that the coracle would collide with the hull. She pushed against the hull to stop the coracle from touching. Reed dropped his bow and pushed as well and the coracle sidled alongside. The Var ship lurched aside at their touch, but not too much. Hopefully on board the vessel it would feel like a wave passing.

Lark pointed at the bow, where an elaborate flag of intertwined snakes whipped in the wind.

This was the lead boat. This boat would be the best guarded of all.

The rower looked at her, questioningly. She motioned to a dark line toward the keel. Slowly, they maneuvered the coracle to it. A rope. The anchor rope, dipping deep down to the sand at the bottom of the bay. They tied the coracle to the line, and Lark whispered, "I'll go first, then the archers, then rowers. Do whatever you can to catch them unawares. Remember, surprise is our weapon."

She took a deep breath, and floated up to the deck. There was a watch, two sleepy looking men facing toward the front of the boat, away from her. All the other men were asleep on the deck itself, wrapped in their cloaks, their shields and axes close to hand. She leaned over the side of the ship and motioned the others to follow her.

Without a sound, she took out the closest Var in his sleep, and then another. She went for a third, but the ship lurched suddenly as her men climbed the anchor rope to join her on deck.

In an instant the deck was in chaos, the watchmen shouting, the sleeping men awakening and tripping over each other as they reached for their weapons.

Behind her Reed the archer was first to climb to the top of the rope. A Var raised his axe to strike him, but Lark's sword swept in an arc and the man fell back in a pool of blood.

She used all her skill, and was soon flying over the enemy, taking out two at a time. They were valiant, but the reputation of the Ariane preceded her, and once they saw her on the deck of their ship, cloaked in silver, with her flashing sword, they froze. The archers picked them off as Lark distracted them. The peasants did what they could, bludgeoning the Var as they lumbered past. A peasant rower fell, cut in two by a Var axe. But between the surprise and the confusion, the archers' arrows and Lark's shining sword, there were at least twenty Var warriors lying on the deck, and the Var leaders were screaming to the sleepy men to reinforce the ranks.

Lark grabbed Reed by the arm. "Now we retreat. We've wounded them so they must withdraw. We can do no better than this. Get the others and head for the boat."

She grabbed the only surviving rower and pulled him toward the ship's side. He was wounded, his arm hanging useless. She dragged him along beside her as he tried to get his feet under him and help.

Suddenly she felt something inside—a horrible blow. It was Fawn. She had been wounded somewhere out there in the fog, and Lark felt it rip into her consciousness. She had never felt such pain.

She doubled over in her tracks. It was hard to separate the terror and pain Fawn felt from what she herself saw before her own eyes. She was lost in a sea of pain and could not focus. A blow to her right arm knocked Lark to her knees. Her cloak deflected the blade, but her arm went numb, and her sword dropped from her hand with a clatter.

Lark looked up to see a Var, apparently their leader from the elaborate gold and jeweled sash he wore, standing in her path. He raised his heavy axe overhead. Her Ariane blade lay at his feet. Lark tried to concentrate, to cut herself off from the pain and confusion coming from Fawn, and focus on the man in front of her.

The Var fell at her feet, an arrow through one eye.

She looked over her shoulder, and Reed stood, bow in hand. "I believe we were retreating, My Lady." He grinned and held out his hand to her. "So you are not invincible, Lady."

Lark did not return the smile. Good Lord, where was Fawn in all this? She grabbed her sword off the deck with her left hand. Her right hand was quickly recovering from the blow and she was able to take Reed's outstretched hand and let him pull her to her feet.

"That man," she said, nodding toward the injured rower. "We can't leave him."

Reed hesitated, "But he is—" He bit back the rest, then hurriedly picked up the man and carried him to the side of the boat.

Lark swung over the side and shimmied down the rope to the

coracle, unable to float with that horror still echoing in her head.

She helped Reed lower the injured rower down, and as soon as his boots hit the boat they were off, rowing back to shore.

Behind them they heard a chant go up among the Var: "Ulik! Ulik!"

The Var prince was dead.

Reed bent over the wounded rower. He pulled off his silk scarf and wrapped it around the gaping injury in the man's arm. "You fought bravely," Reed told him.

Lark turned away from him, unable to think of anything except getting to shore and finding Fawn.

Lark ignored the pain in her arm, and she and the other archer rowed as fast as they could. How bad was the injury? It could not be too bad, Lark told herself. She had broken the connection with Fawn, but it was only pain and shock she had felt, not her death.

When the boat finally ground to shore, Lark jumped out and ran up the beach.

Lotus stood on the gravel, looking down at a small silver-clad figure.

Lark knelt on the ground. A Var spear had torn away Fawn's back. Fawn had pushed her cloak back over her shoulders, leaving herself unprotected. It was a childish mistake, but the cloak was heavy, and hot, and in the heat of battle Fawn had forgotten her training.

"Never leave my back unprotected," Fawn whispered.

Tears filled Lark's eyes. Of course she had forgotten. She was just a child, a dreamer who was not meant for battle. In the fear and chaos around her she had forgotten her lessons. Lark felt a rage at Willow well up inside her. Why had she sent Fawn into battle when she was so unprepared?

"Pray for me, Lark," Fawn whispered. Lark knew which words she wanted, but she could not say them aloud, not in this company. She nodded at Fawn. "I will say the proper words for you." She held Fawn's hand, and with her cloak covering their hands, she made the sign of the triangle in Fawn's palm.

Fawn closed her eyes and smiled.

"You will see the Afterlife, Sister," Lark said aloud. "The Gods will recognize you in your shining raiment, and the Gatekeeper will let you cross over to the other side, where all your wishes will be fulfilled, and you will serve the royal family in glory forever." Lord take this child into your care. She is of good heart and has received your words in secret as all believers do. She has prayed with me in the night in our chamber, and has recited the creed of our one God. Welcome her into Heaven, Oh Lord, and let her rest in peace.

Lark cradled Fawn's head in her lap. The short silver hair was soft under her hands. Fawn had been her only friend, the only one who didn't care that Lark was not of noble birth. Fawn had offered friendship to her, had even looked up to her, not caring that Lark was by all rights her inferior by birth. Lark unclasped the ruby pearl necklace from her own neck, and laid it in Fawn's hands.

"We won!" Reed's cheerful voice cut into her thoughts. He looked down and saw what Lark held in her lap.

Fawn was gone, and only God knew where her spirit was now.

Reed fell to his knees beside Lark. He sobbed, and gently touched Fawn's hair. Lark instinctively gasped at his audacity in touching an Ariane, then realized. Lark stared. Täryn. Of course. The castle by the sea where Fawn climbed trees and her older brother carried her on his shoulders. She had known Fawn but had not known her.

Reed bowed his head. "I will take her home. She will lie in our family tomb."

"I am sorry, Reed. She must stay with us."

He flared at that. "She was my sister before she was Ariane, My Lady."

"I know. But she will be buried in the catacombs next to the kings of the Silver Isle. It is the duty of an Ariane."

Reed stood abruptly, fists clenched. He said nothing for a moment, then in that cool voice she already knew, said only, "very well, Ariane." He turned on his heel and left.

Mouse landed on a pile of hard sticks that tumbled around him with a clatter.

He was in complete darkness.

Just when he caught his breath, Oxen landed on top of him with a thud.

Ox got to his feet and hauled Mouse up beside him. Mouse could hear him fumbling over something in the darkness.

"I can't see," Mouse said.

"You don't want to see."

Mouse tried to move forward, his arms out in front of him. He touched something, a stick, long and thin, and then the crash echoed on and on for ages.

"Stand still. Make another sound and I'll cut you down here."

Soon he heard the sharp strike of stone on metal, and the accompanying flash as a spark momentarily flared in front of them. It happened again and again, until, finally, the torch was lit.

"Put the light out!" Mouse cried. "Oh, Ox. Put it out!"

In a rare moment of sympathy, Oxen held Mouse to him and let him cry against his chest.

"They are no longer suffering." Oxen's voice was rough, as if he too held back tears.

All around them lay bodies. Bones. The bones of people. Every skull a person, hundreds of them. All scattered about, some with rags of clothing on them and dried skin stretched thinly over the bones like paper, some just white bone, bare on the ground and in crevices in the walls of the cave. For that was where they were. A cave, its ceiling lost in shadow far above their heads, its walls smooth rock, all black. Everywhere black, with veins of shimmering silver like lightning frozen into the stone walls all around them.

The bodies were not shrouded and laid to rest in respectful burial, but lay as dried out shells of people, contorted, skin withered against the skulls in expressions of fear and pain.

Finally Mouse pulled back from Ox and opened his eyes again.

He saw that not all in the room was ugly and evil, for in the center, surrounded by death, was a beautiful golden box, big enough to hold a grown-up person's body. The box was all covered in golden metal, maybe real gold, Mouse thought, though he had never seen real gold. The gold was all inlaid with glittering silvery moths made of some metal like the streaks of silver in the stone walls. The moth's eyes were of sapphires, and the torchlight made them seem to move and follow him like something alive. Mouse looked down, feeling it was very wrong to see all the horrible bodies surrounding that lovely box.

At Mouse's feet lay a man, eyes closed, not in serenity but with fear frozen on the face.

Mouse had to look away.

"Come," Ox said roughly. "We must move on."

"But I don't understand." Mouse looked down at the man. "What did he die of?"

"Religion." Oxen spat the word.

Mouse moved gingerly through the sea of bodies. "There are so many of them."

"One-hundred and twenty-three."

"How long have they been here?"

"Fifteen years, boy."

"Does Master Raven know about this?"

Oxen looked at him funny. "He knows." He looked around at the walls. "These are worshippers of the peasants' God, for all the good it did them. The old king buried his wife fifteen years ago and grew angry because no one wanted to be buried with her."

"You mean after they died. What difference would it make?"

"Not after they died, Mouse," Ox said gently. "The king believed he was a god, and must be worshipped as one. The people were supposed to think it was a privilege"—he spat the word—"to be buried with royalty. The peasant god was a rebellion the likes of which had never been seen. The simple words, 'there is no god but God,' were the most treasonous words ever spoken in the Silver Isle. The king believed 'I am the word and the only path to the afterlife' was literally true, and did not accept that his subjects believed otherwise."

Mouse didn't understand, and focused on the part that he could grasp. "Master Raven said that stuff about the path before. He said it like it was a bad thing."

Oxen looked at him. "Standing in this tomb, you doubt it is a bad thing?"

"Then you believe in the one true God, Ox? You always said it was stupid."

"It is stupid. I believe in nothing."

"Except Master Raven," Mouse said with certainty.

"Yes," Ox said quietly. "I believe in him."

"Did Master Raven know about this?"

"Mouse, Master Raven's father was the king."

Mouse tried to absorb that. "Did Master Raven believe he was god, too?"

"No. When he was a boy he spoke up to try to make his father stop doing things like this. The king was angry. But Raven was his son. He could beat him, but Raven was still his son. Unless the king wanted to kill his wife and son, there was nothing he could do about their words."

"His wife?"

"Raven's mother—the king's wife—believed in the peasant god, and taught Raven to believe, too. She would go down into the city and worship the peasant god with the people, in secret."

"Did you go, too?" He asked Ox, wondering how he knew all this.

"No." He looked away.

He took Ox's calloused hand in his. "Do you have a friend who went to the meetings and told you about it?" he asked.

Ox pulled his hand away and wiped his eyes. "Dust in here," he said.

He looked at something over in the corner, then held the torch high and went over there. He knelt by one of the bodies. It must have been a woman from the clothing—old, raggedy peasant clothes. Next to her lay a smaller skeleton, even smaller than Mouse.

Mouse went closer. Ox knelt down by the bodies. Something gleamed in the torchlight, on the front of the gown.

Oxen reached out one hand, trembling, and took hold of the gleam—a necklace, with a dangling charm wrought out of some base metal, depicting the triad of the peasant God.

Oxen closed his fist around the charm, then yanked it, and it came free. He threw it into a corner, where it landed with a jingle of metal on stone that echoed loudly in the tomb.

He stood back up, then just stared down at the two bodies for a long time.

Finally he turned away from the skeletons, and the shadow of the torch moved across the floor with him, lighting the scatter of the child's bones at Mouse's feet.

At Mouse's feet he saw one of the "sticks" had fallen away, off by itself on the floor. He bent to pick it up. A bone smaller than his own arm. He placed it with the rest of the body it had come from, next to the small skull.

"He was four years old," Oxen said gruffly, finally breaking his silence.

Then Ox straightened up and looked around, as if making a decision. "If you don't want to join him, keep quiet and do as I say."

"How can we go back up?"

"We can't. There is no way out of the burial shaft. This is a tomb, boy. No one gets out of here alive."

Oxen raised the torch.

"So how do we get out of here?"

"Look for the sign of God." Ox raised his torch and began exploring the cave, picking his way over the jumble of bodies.

"Which God?"

"The God that got all these people killed—your God, Mouse."

Mouse looked down at the bones of the little boy at his feet. His clothes were still partially intact, and he still had a bit of hair. The face was not just a skull, but had skin, like parchment, with eyelids pale silk paper over the holes. He still had eyelashes. He had been alive, breathing and feeling and thinking like any real person, and the king had murdered him. And Master Raven was the king's son.

"Is Master Raven in trouble because of what happened here?"

"I don't know, Mouse. He is in trouble. And we must get him away from the people who believe in killing like this. Now shut up and look."

Behind the boy's head Mouse saw a thin line in brown on the wall.

Mouse carefully moved the boy's bones. He laid him down on the floor with great tenderness.

"Don't mess with him, boy! Leave him in peace. Get away from there."

Mouse pointed at the wall. The mark was clear, where the boy's head had rested. Three interlaced shapes formed the triad of the one true God: past, present and future.

With a cry, Oxen passed him the torch and then dropped to his knees and began digging frantically in the dirt at the base of the wall. "So close," he kept muttering. "They were so close."

Soon Ox brought up a small something in his palm.

He handed it to Mouse. It was a metal key, long and notched and very rusty.

"What is it?"

"It's our way out."

Raven heard muffled shouting.

He made his way to the prison door and set his ear to the wood.

Suddenly, the voices came closer and he could hear the words being spoken.

"We have done nothing, My Lady. I swear it." It was a woman, terrified, and Raven heard the cry of a baby nearby.

"Nothing? You were at a treasonous meeting." The female voice (Ariane?) sounded bored, unconcerned about the frightened woman and infant.

"It was not treason. We only met to speak together about...."

"—About your God? The one that says you are equal to me and my kind, and that you may refuse any order the Lady Steward gives you?"

The baby continued to sob quietly, its cries perhaps muffled against the woman's chest. "But we meant no harm. Please. My children—please let us go."

"Why do you cry, woman? You will be meeting your god very soon."

The voices faded as they moved off past his door.

The sweat broke out on his chest, and he shivered as the horror swept over him. No more deaths. Not again.

He heard doors banging shut far away, and more distant cries. He laid his palms against the smooth wood of his prison door. This could not be happening again.

How could he have thought this wasn't his problem? Lark was right. He must do something. He felt so stupidly helpless. He hadn't realized his responsibility until it was too late to save them—or even himself.

He heard soft footsteps again down the hall.

He banged his fists against the door.

The steps stopped. "What do you want?" The voice was female, the one who had taken the woman and child away.

"I must see Lark—she is one of you."

"One of us?"

"She is—" he tried to think back, remember the brooch she wore. "She is Number Six. I must see her."

The guard laughed, and walked away.

Raven banged his fists on the door until they bled, but no one came.

XV

They had done it. The small group of cobbled-together Ariane, noble archers, and peasant footmen had defeated a Var attack. It was unheard-of, and a lesson in how to use their own strength against the Var's weakness. Lark's first command, and she had set a precedent. With only one Ariane casualty.

Lark bowed her head.

The Var had lost a battle, and they had retreated. For how long? Who knew, but at least there would be peace for a while now, while the Var returned to their distant land and licked their wounds.

But the price? Little Fawn was dead. Lark was now alone among the Ariane. Fawn had been her only friend, save the Lady Willow herself. But the Lady would always see her as a child, while Fawn had seen her as, what? Not a peasant. Not beneath her. Simply as a friend. Now she was truly alone.

The whole thing had been wrong. Little Fawn deserved better. She never should have been sent to fight. She was unprepared. Why had the Lady Willow sent her? It seemed so illogical, to send Lark as the leader when no one trusted her, and Fawn as a soldier when she was the worst fighter among them. Willow always had a plan, but this one made no sense.

She pulled aside the flap on the main tent. All the others were outside, busy with the tasks Lotus had set them of bandaging their wounds, making a meager meal of their rice cakes and wine, and wrapping the body of their little Ariane sister for the return to Chÿar.

Lark could face none of these tasks, and Lotus had the business well in hand. She would let her belligerent sister take the authority—and the glory. She herself needed to sleep, to put off thinking about the changes this day had wrought.

The pallets were all empty, lined up against the side of the tent. Lark took off her cloak and sword and carefully laid them aside, then flopped down on a pallet and closed her eyes. She tried to will herself to go to sleep, but sleep did not come.

Not long after, someone else entered the darkened tent, another Ariane from the swish of the cloak. Lark didn't look up.

"Are you awake?" It was Lotus, sounding even more sullen and distant than usual.

She opened her eyes. "Not now, Sister. It's been a bad day."

"You won the battle." It was the nicest thing Lotus had ever said to her, made incongruous by the sword she had drawn.

Lark sat up on the pallet. Lotus stood at the end of the bed, in First Stance, sword drawn and forward, cloak on her free arm, ready to be swung into defense.

"That's not funny, Lotus."

"You did well," Lotus said, again with that subdued tone that belied the aggressive posture.

"I'd appreciate the compliments more if you weren't waving your sword in my direction, Lotus."

But Lotus wasn't waving her sword. She was holding it in First Stance. First Stance was the position for preparation to attack against a skilled opponent, as the Rule stated. Surely she was joking.

Lark raised her hands, palms out. "I am unarmed, Sister," she said. She tried to make a joke of it.

Lotus didn't smile. "I am not your sister."

Lark lay back against the pallet and stared at the ceiling. "Of course you aren't. Let's not go into that again. You are noble-born, and I was born a slave far beneath your station. We have no dispute over that. My status in the Ariane is something for you to discuss with the Lady herself, not me. This is not the time to settle our differences." Lark rolled over and closed her eyes.

"This is the only time, Lark."

Lark sat up again. Lotus was not joking. She realized the sword in her hand was not still—worse, it shook just slightly from the white-knuckled grip with which she held it. Lark had never seen that before from Lotus. Emotion affecting her grip. What emotion? Lotus had always been cooly superior. She was not cool at all right now.

Lark tried again: "As I said, this is something to discuss later, after we've slept. Take it up with the Lady."

"I have." Lotus took a step forward, to the very edge of the pallet, and the sword blade hovered far-too near Lark's head for comfort.

"What are you talking about?" Her own sword was tucked next to the pallet. But of course Lotus would know that. "You act possessed, Lotus."

"What possessed you, Lark?" Lotus was really shaking now, with anger and, maybe, fear? "The Lady treated you like her own daughter. You were her favorite, though there were others of us far more worthy. You should have been grateful. What have you done?"

Lark stood up on the pallet, grabbing for her sheathed sword as she rose. She pulled the sword from its sheath and faced Lotus, the pallet raising her to be almost Lotus's height even barefoot. "You have gone mad. What have I done? You tell me. I have no idea what you are talking about."

The two faced each other in silence for a moment. Lotus seemed rattled in a way Lark had never seen before. If she was plotting the murder of her long-time rival, she was hardly enjoying it.

"Lotus, speak to me. You are raising a sword against a sister—like it or not, I am a sister in the Ariane. This is against all training. You are not challenging me for my place—you rank above me. I have committed no crime against the Rule. You have no right to attack me like this."

"You broke the Rule."

"Oh, Lotus, stop it! By your standards, any minor infraction of the Rule is a grave sin punishable by death. What did I do? Place my left foot ahead of my right in temple last time? Use the wrong whetstone to polish my hand knife? I think the Lady Willow would disapprove of you killing me for that."

Lotus's eyes narrowed. "You think so?"

"The Lady? You are standing here claiming that the Lady Willow told you to fight me?"

"Not to fight you. To kill you. But even you deserve the chance to defend yourself. I will not run you through in your sleep. So raise your sword." Lotus looked angry, and formidable, and genuinely frightened. She was not joking at all.

Lark raised her sword in the first defense posture. The pallet was uneven, its straw filling making for unsteady footing. "You must have misunderstood her, Lotus. As you said, I am her favorite. Why would she want me killed?" The last thing Willow would want is for Lark to die just after fulfilling her promise to bring the prince back from exile. Did she dare tell Lotus about Prince Raven? Would it anger her even more to know what a great gift Lark had brought Willow?

"You plotted against the Lady. Don't think it is a secret. Everyone knows you meet with peasant rebels late at night. It's been known for years. You tried to bring Fawn into your plot, taking her to your secret meetings."

"Fawn is—was—innocent. She did nothing wrong."

"And she died as she should have, honorably in battle. As you should have."

Lark felt horror wash over her. "My God, Lotus. She was a child. What did you do?"

Lotus looked tortured. "I did nothing to Fawn. You were supposed to die. Both of you. This battle would have been an honorable end, and no one would have to know of your terrible crimes. But now, your treachery must be stopped."

"What treachery? I took Fawn to a peasant religious meeting.

Yes, I confess. We marked our bread and we read the words of the peasant God. We did nothing to harm the Lady or the Ariane. The Lady has always known about me, and you cannot tell me she ordered the death of me, or Fawn. Fawn. Oh, how could you, Lotus?"

"I did not kill Fawn. Thank the gods she was killed honorably in battle. She will be buried with honor, and no one need know her part in this treachery. But you—why didn't you die in battle, Lark? You could have died with honor, saved from this shameful end."

Lotus's sword rose in the first attack, and Lark responded automatically in defense. This could not be happening. She thought of Prince Raven, even now with Willow. Would she never see him take the throne? Would she never see him again? She tried to keep Lotus talking. "What treachery, Lotus? You must explain yourself before running me through. This is some kind of mistake." Lotus really thought her worship of the peasant's God for the past fifteen years was a crime worth killing over? Why now?

"Mistake? Yes, it was a mistake for the Lady to give a slave the honor of joining the Ariane. And it was a mistake for you to plot to destroy the Ariane. Did you think you could bring that spy into the Lady's chamber without her knowing? He will die, and so will you. Then we will be clean of this treachery."

"Spy?" Lark pictured that handsome man who met with Willow, their heads bowed together so intimately. She had never questioned Willow about the relationship. But if Lotus thought he was some enemy spy.... "Lotus, I have nothing to do with Wolf. He is Willow's —friend—not mine."

"The other one," Lotus said coldly. She was beginning to calm down now, and that made her dangerous. "The crippled one."

Lark felt the room spin around her. No, it couldn't be true. Raven. Alone in the city and branded a spy. When she found her voice, she asked, "Have you seen this spy?"

Lotus shook her head. "I did not see him myself, but I was told about him."

"Told by whom?" When Lotus didn't answer, Lark shouted it:

"By whom?"

"Our Lady, of course."

No. Not Willow. Lark felt her world crumble around her. Raven was dead. She had taken him from safety and led him like a lamb to slaughter. Slaughter by the woman who had saved her own life.

She spoke in a hoarse whisper: "This spy is a tall man, with silver hair, a patch over his eye, and a limp?"

Lotus nodded. "A poor choice for an assassin, don't you think, Lark? He could hardly outfight a peasant, let alone an Ariane."

Lark thought of Raven's sword stance on that cliff in Rïal. "You would be surprised at what he could do, Lotus."

"Willow told me he barely put up a fight when confronted."

"I know that's not true, Lotus. I have seen him hold a sword. He could defend himself in any honorable battle—but not against treachery. Not against Ariane." Then she realized the worst of it: "Willow? Willow told you this?"

"Of course." Lotus's sword was not shaking now. "And she gave me orders to kill all involved in the plot."

She lunged at Lark suddenly, looking for the quick kill. Lark raised her sword instinctively and parried the blow, letting it slide harmlessly against the flat side of her own blade.

"I am not cloaked, Lotus! This is hardly a fair fight."

"I am not fighting you, Lark. I am killing you."

Lark jumped over Lotus and landed behind, but Lotus turned and met her as she landed, thrusting again at Lark's unprotected side.

Lark stepped aside. "I am not going to kill you, Lotus. You have been lied to."

"Shut up and fight."

"Lotus, you must listen. The man I brought back is not a spy. He is Raven himself."

"Nonsense. Everyone knows he is dead."

"No. I found him, as the Lady charged me to."

"Willow knew Raven. She was guard to his family when he was young. She would know if he was the true prince."

"Yes, Lotus. She would."

Lotus stopped. Again the sword wavered. Lark saw her opening for the quick kill but did not take it. Lotus had been lied to as much as she herself had been. She waited and watched Lotus's face.

"You are claiming she knows?" Lotus whispered.

Lark thought of the tears in Willow's eyes when Lark arrived with the prince. She thought of the raid on the peasant service, and of Willow's hand on the spy Wolf. She thought of poor little Fawn, sent into battle unprepared, and of her own first command at such an inappropriate time. "Yes, Lotus," she said with certainty. "She must know."

"Why? Why would she do such a thing? You are lying to save yourself."

"Why would I, Lotus? As you have said, I am Ariane. It is all I am. Without it, I am nothing but a homeless slave. I was given this gift by the Lady herself. Why would I plot against her? To be Ariane is my whole world. You know this is true."

Lotus nodded almost imperceptibly.

"And you know I saw Raven leave the massacre when I was a child. I told everyone this. It is no secret."

Again the small nod.

"The Lady Willow gave me leave to travel on a quest to find the missing prince. Even if he were not Raven, he would not be an assassin, but just a man I have mistaken for the prince. I would not be a traitor, but a fool."

"But that would mean the lady—"

She stopped, unable to say it, so Lark finished the damning sentence: "—wants the prince of the Silver Isle dead, and is using you to cover her plot."

"It is treason."

Lark nodded. "It is treason. And it is murder. Think about it, Lotus. I bring a crippled man of noble birth to see the Lady? As you said, he is hardly a suitable assassin. But he is exactly what I have described for all these years—a wounded boy, limping away bloody and battered from the burning castle."

Lotus took a step back.

Lark returned to the first defensive posture, and waited.

Silence. A long silence, while Lotus went over everything in her mind. "No one else must know. The Ariane guards—they would not hold the prince prisoner if they knew—it is a blasphemy—how could the lady commit a blasphemy—she led the service—she would die in shame—it cannot be...."

"Lotus?"

"I do not believe you."

Lark raised her sword again, preparing to battle Lotus to the death.

Lotus lowered her own sword to her side. "I do not believe you, but I must see for myself. We will speak to this crippled, silver-haired man in the dungeon before he is executed."

They had all returned to the city, nobles and Ariane escorting the body of Fawn in solemn procession. Lark had chafed at the slowness, anxious to get back and get Raven out of prison as soon as possible, but Lotus refused to bend the rules, and would not leave behind the nobles, nor let Lark ride on ahead.

Finally they arrived. Leaving Fawn's body with the others, Lark, with Lotus a silent shadow, rushed for the prison.

"Raven!" The door of his prison swung open and Lark rushed inside. He blinked up against the bright light. From where he sat in the corner of his cell, she was just a silhouette in the doorway.

Then his vision cleared, and it was her, and he had never been so glad to see anyone in his life. She looked terrible.

Her clothing was stained with what looked like dried blood, and there were dark circles under her eyes. She seemed haunted, and rushed to him almost as if she wanted him to take her in his arms. He instinctively reached out for her as she knelt before him on the floor.

"You are unharmed, Your Grace?"

Never had he been happier to be called that. "I am not injured."

He felt the twinge in his back where he had been struck. "Not much, anyway."

Lark put her arms around him and helped him to his feet. Once he was standing, she did not take her arm away, but continued to hold on to him, almost as if for comfort. He placed his own arm around her waist, and felt the warmth of her as a balm to his bruised courage.

"Help me get him out of here," Lark said. Raven saw that another Ariane was standing in the doorway, staring at him in disbelief.

The other one narrowed her eyes at him. "You are the man Lark brought back to the city?"

He held his head up high. "I am Raven yr Griffon, Ariane. You have much to answer for. It is a violation of the Book of Rule to raise a hand to me."

Lark started at that statement, but the other said only, "Perhaps."

Raven wanted to smack the arrogant one. "Perhaps? I am Griffon, and you serve me."

Lark seemed surprised by his words, but he didn't have time to play games. If he was going to pay the price for being Griffon, he damned well would insist on the respect that went with it. Being bashed in the neck and thrown in prison was not appropriate Ariane behavior, and he wouldn't stand for it.

"Come on, Lotus," Lark said. "We haven't much time."

Lotus shook her head. "I will not commit treason against the Lady Willow."

Lark let go of Raven and lunged for the door, but the other Ariane was as quick as she was, and the door slammed shut before Lark could reach it.

"Lotus!" she cried.

Raven heard the bolts in the door slam home, and the muffled voice on the other side say, "I must see what the Lady has to say before I decide. I cannot break my vows for this alleged royal without proof."

Raven slid back down to the floor, and put his head in his hands for a minute. They were once again trapped in the dimness, but at least he was not alone anymore. As sorry as he was to entangle Lark in his problems, he had felt the loss of her keenly these last few days.

"It's nice to know you aren't evil as I feared you were, Lark. But I take it we have lost another battle."

She didn't reply. He watched her back.

Lark stood for a while, her head bent, her palms spread against the door. Eventually she came over, her quicksilver cloak jingling as she sat down next to him. "I am sorry, My Prince. I never should have brought you here."

"You are now prisoner, too."

"I am Ariane. My life is forfeit. Your life is more valuable than mine."

"No one's life is more valuable than another's, Lark. I said that fifteen years ago, as someone has recently reminded me." He smiled gently at the memory of her fiery challenge—was it only days ago?

"But you said you no longer believed that."

Raven suddenly realized how much his feelings had changed since meeting Lark. "I was wrong. A Griffon heir must tell the truth. Not because he is better, or wiser, or chosen by the gods. But because someone must tell the truth, to serve as the voice of reason against this sort of insanity. It is necessary. And it is my fate."

Lark furrowed her brow at him. "What did you mean, I wasn't as evil as you feared?"

"Just that." He rubbed his sore hands against his breeches, then picked up the rock he had dropped when the door had burst open. He began to chip away again at the obsidian wall, where he had already excavated a small hole. "You will find the door hinges will not budge, my dear. This is my latest project. Pick up a rock and join me. We have plenty of time."

She stared at him. "You really thought I was evil?"

He chuckled. "You brought me here at swordpoint, blustering all the while about killing Oxen and little Mouse, and then someone cracked me on the neck and I woke up in the Ariane prison. What was I to think?"

She scouted around for a rock and then knelt down by him and began chipping at the wall. "You know I was never going to hurt Ox and Mouse."

"Of course. On some level I always knew that."

"The evil was Willow all along." Her voice cracked as if this admission cost her something.

"It was not Willow who hit me. It was a man's voice I heard."

She pondered that for a bit. "Wolf," she said. "He is her lover."

"Lover?" He kept working on the hole. "The Ariane have changed since I was last here. Do you all take lovers?"

She blushed at that, and looked away. "Of course not, Your Grace." She stopped tapping and looked at the wall. "This is not going to work."

"When you come up with another plan, let me know. In the meantime this is the best one I have."

"I am sorry, Your Grace."

"Raven." He reached up with one grimy hand and brushed a strand of her black hair from her cheek. "Protocol no longer matters, Lark. We can be honest now."

She sighed and leaned her head against his hand. He held her cheek, cupped there against his palm. Then he pulled his hand away and turned to face the wall, tapping again with the rock. The longing to touch someone still welled up inside him like a hunger that never was satisfied. It was illegal to touch him—though Lark had already violated that taboo several times.

Why some fool had decreed that royalty must not make contact with peasants, he could not fathom. A childhood in which no one but his blood relatives ever touched him had been isolating and lonely. The first time a peasant child touched him was a shock. It had been in the back of a dank cellar during a peasant service. The other boy had punched him in the arm after he won the tessera game. Everyone in the room had fallen silent, but Raven had laughed and punched him back, and his mother had smiled, and they went on from there. Later he had traded with the other boy—

the small pendant of black pearl he always wore on a gold chain for the boy's triad symbol of carved wood on a leather thong. It had seemed a fine trade at the time, but his mother made him give it back. The necklace was the younger son's pearl, and had for centuries symbolized a boy's status as second in line for the throne of the House of Griffon. "We will not speak of this to your father," Mother had whispered, and he had known that lives hung in the balance of that silence.

"We will find a way, Your Grace," Lark said, misinterpreting his silence. "We will get you out of here and you can return to your old life in Rïal. I was wrong to force you to come here, I see that now."

He didn't have the heart to tell her that Rïal was gone for him. There had been no going back since the moment she recognized him on that hill outside the inn. But that was not necessarily a bad thing, he now realized. He looked over at her, an expression on her face of guilt and shame.

He needed to make her understand what she had done for him. He took a deep breath, like a swimmer about to plunge into water far over his head. "No, Lark. Not Rïal. Rïal is in the past. I do not want to be king. I did not choose this role. But you were right. We are under attack by the Var. There is poverty, and great danger to the people. And there is corruption in high places."

He watched her face, as she looked at him wonderingly. "I am the heir to the Griffon throne. I do not have to like it, but this is the fate God has given me. I cannot hide from my responsibility any more. I am here, though I did not wish to be, and I must do what I can to make things right." He swallowed hard, then said the words he had denied for fifteen years. "I am Raven yr Griffon, King of the Silver Isle, and Holder of the Shepherd's Sapphire Scepter."

"But they will kill you."

He nodded. "Probably. People die every day. But I will not die quietly. Will you stand beside me, Lark?"

She smiled. "I have my role, too, My Prince. I will stand beside you."

Suddenly he leaned toward her and brushed his lips across hers.

Her mouth was warm, and she tasted of everything he had longed for all his life. It was agony to end the kiss and pull away.

"What did you do that for?" she asked when she caught her breath.

"Royal prerogative," he whispered, and kissed her again.

XVI

One of his hands went to her waist and began to raise her tunic.

"I have never...," she looked down at her hand, still intertwined in his.

"Of course," he said softly. He dropped his hands and turned away, taking a deep, ragged breath. "I should not have pushed you."

Lark reached for him. "I have never before," she whispered, her mouth against his. "Until now."

She closed her eyes and felt his breath on her skin. *I love you, My Prince,* she wanted to say, but there was no point. There was no escape from within the Ariane prison. She realized that now. No matter why this had happened, no matter what had made Willow turn against her vows, it was too late. The Ariane sisters would come soon, on orders from the Lady Willow, and Lark would fight them to the last.

She would die defending the prince, but she would lose against the others of the forty-four. And then Raven too would die. And there was nothing she could do about it. She had murdered the Prince of the Silver Isle through her gullibility and brash decisions.

She lay back against the pallet and pulled his body over her, wrapping herself around him. He probably thought her tears were from the pain of her first time with a man. She let him think it, and held him tighter.

Mouse followed Ox down yet another underground hall. After days of searching the catacombs, hiding from the guards and trying to find a way to get to where Master Prince Raven was at, Mouse was sure they were lost. Ox had taken to muttering to himself more, and he had thrown away the torch, so they wandered in the dark.

The walls around them were seamed with the same silvery metallic gleam Mouse had seen in the tomb. Everything was black, a shiny black stone that reflected the light of the torch across the walls. Anyone in the tunnel would see them coming when they used the torch, so Ox had cast it aside and they felt their way along, pausing at each fork while Ox pondered the options.

They heard tapping faintly down one dark path. "Not that way," Ox muttered. "That's the forge. Too many Ariane down there."

"Where they make the swords?"

"Yes." Ox felt his way along, then after a long time, stepped out into the middle of the tunnel. "Where is everybody?" he whispered.

"I don't know."

"I wasn't asking you, boy. There should be guards here, all through this area. The forge is that way, and the prison is down there. Up ahead climbs up to the the main level and the temple. But no one's down here. What is that witch up to?"

"Lark?"

"Someone worse than Lark."

"But where is everybody?"

"I truly don't know. We might be too late."

Mouse tried to rush past him into the tunnel leading to the prison. "Too late to save Master Prince Raven? But we have to save him!"

Ox grabbed him by the tunic and held him back. "This isn't a fairy tale, boy. There won't be a happy ending." Ox leaned against the wall and put his head down.

Mouse saw shadows arcing across the tunnel ahead. Someone was coming from the prison with a light. He pulled on Ox, and they ran quickly, dashing along the path that led up to the main level. They kept moving, staying a corner ahead of the torchlit figure coming behind them.

They came out of the darkness into a huge room filled with people. The room was larger than anything Mouse had ever seen. His first impression was of light. Light glittered everywhere. Huge candles gave off a strong clear glow of purest white that flooded the place with a light like a bright sunny day.

After the days spent in darkness in the catacombs the light made his vision blur and his eyes water. He blinked hard, trying to clear his sight.

"This way." Ox pulled him toward a group of peasants huddled at a doorway. The opening led into a room even bigger than the one they were in, and the people were being instructed in how to behave once they went inside.

"Keep your heads down and your mouths closed," the lady Ariane guard ordered. "You are going to see great things, and you will tell all your fellows about them when you leave."

Ox sidled up to an arthritic looking servingwoman, her ragged gown a sharp contrast to the splendid mural on the wall behind her.

"What great things?" Ox whispered to her.

"Where you been, old man? You best look sharp. The Ariane are in a ripe mood tonight."

"Why?" Ox asked.

"Quiet!" an Ariane ordered. She was not quite as tall as Lark, and her hair was a brilliant silver braid down her back. She looked mean, and didn't have the twinkle in her eye that Lark always did.

Ox bowed his head humbly to the Ariane. Funny how he could make himself look scared like the others, when Mouse could see from the way Ox clenched his fists that he was angry. Mouse wondered how much practice it took to bow to people you hated.

Ox saw Mouse's expression and pulled him closer. "Unruffle your feathers, boy. This is not the time for your sass."

The crowd began to surge forward as the Ariane ushered them through the doorway and into the big room. Ox nudged the old woman again. "Tell me," he whispered.

"The funeral of a dead Ariane," she whispered back. "We were ordered here."

Mouse saw Ox's shoulders relax. "One of them died?" he asked.

She nodded. "The Var got one of the she-devils." She turned her head and spat on the beautiful floor. "Praise be the Lady Willow," she added loudly with a glance at the guards.

They entered the main room, pushed from behind by the crowd following them. Mouse had never seen such a magnificent room. Everywhere were pretty statues, and beautiful tiles lay on the floor. The ceiling arched up into great beams that seemed to be carved out of ivory.

But in the middle of the room was one of those coffins like the one with the moths he had seen before, and it took the fun out of seeing such a beautiful room. Mouse wondered who was inside of the box, waiting to be put in the catacombs, and he thought it must be someone very good, since so many people were gathering to say goodbye to her. Oxen didn't seem to care about the Ariane in the coffin, but he seemed very interested in seeing all the other Ariane who were gathering in the temple.

"This is our chance, boy," he whispered to Mouse.

The temple was full of people. In the fancy part of the main room stood rows of rich people. They were all dressed in fine clothes of velvet and silk the likes of which Mouse had never seen. They looked like a rustling field of flowers in many different colors, but they all seemed sad about the funeral.

Behind a screen where he and Oxen stood, bunches of regular people were gathered. They were mumbling about being called away from work to come to this ceremony. Apparently they had been told they would be in trouble if they didn't show up. They didn't seem to care who was in the golden box.

In the main room, off to one side, another group of regular people stood, but they were wearing chains around their wrists and ankles, and they looked really worried. Mouse saw a boy a little older than him, with a red, sore hand that looked like it must hurt a lot. He watched the boy for a long time, wondering why those people in their poor clothes were in the big room, instead of back behind the screen like the rest of them. They didn't look like they fit. The rich people looked so fine, and the Ariane ladies were so beautiful in their silvery outfits. The rich people looked like they belonged in the beautiful, colorful room. The poor people in chains seemed out of place, like dirt marring a fine gown. Mouse wondered what crimes the people had committed to be in chains.

He noticed Oxen was not paying any attention to them. He was watching the Ariane, muttering to himself. "Thirty-seven, and they're still arriving."

He took Mouse by the hand. "Come on." He pulled him toward the door, bumping through the crowd.

"You can't leave." Another guard, a man this time, stood at the exit, barring Mouse and Oxen's way out.

Ox put on an innocent expression that almost made Mouse laugh—it was so unlike his usual scowl. "My boy needs to relieve himself," he told the guard confidentially. "He will not be able to last through the service, and it would be an embarassment...."

Mouse took the hint. He quickly put his hands down to cover his privates, and bounced on one foot. "Hurry, Papa!" he whined.

The guard looked disgusted, and took a step back. "Get out," he said.

Oxen pulled Mouse out the door, and Mouse noticed the flicker of a smile on his face.

They had fallen asleep. Lark awoke to find herself leaning against Raven on the cold floor, his body a warm and inviting pillow for her head, his arm draped across her back. It was dark in the prison, evening again perhaps, but there was enough moonlight through the high window for her to see the ghostly silver hair of the man lying next to her. She reached up a hand to caress it, but then froze.

She could hear the bolt on the prison door sliding back.

Lark was on her feet before Raven even lifted his head. She fumbled on the floor for her scabbard and then ran to the door. She would not go down without a fight. The door swung outward with a creak and she had her sword out and against the jailer's throat in an instant.

"You should have disarmed me before locking me in," she said. But the man at the door was no Ariane.

Old Oxen stood stock-still, framed in the light from the hallway, a tiny trickle of blood at his neck where she had nicked him before realizing who he was.

"We're rescuing you!" Mouse said, grabbing for her sword arm and missing. "Don't kill us!"

She lowered her sword with hands that shook and Ox took a step back.

The man grabbed at his neck. She looked at him sheepishly. "You are lucky my reflexes were fast enough to stop the stroke, Old One."

"My name is Oxen, you chit," he said hoarsely, his hand still at his throat. "Stop calling me 'Old One.'"

"Master Prince Raven," Mouse whispered loudly, running past her into the prison. "We're rescuing you!"

The child helped Raven to his feet. Raven's walking stick had been lost somewhere, but Ox had found a stake in the catacombs which he had added to his arsenal of weapons. Raven used that as a cane and soon they were all on their feet and ready to go.

"Where are the guards?" Lark asked Ox, peering out into the empty hall.

"They are all at some ceremony in the temple. We could not get past the guards before, but now they've all headed that way. They are all in a raging fit back there—looks almost like a royal funeral. We had better get out of here in case they're thinking of making you the guest of honor, My Lord."

Raven shook his head. "It's not for me. Once again they are holding a state funeral for someone who would not wish it."

Lark felt the tears spring to her eyes as she realized what he was saying. "Fawn?"

"I'm sorry, Lark." Raven took her hand. "There's nothing we can do for her now."

"A bunch of people are there," Mouse piped up. "A little boy there had a sore hand all burned but the soldiers wouldn't let him sit down."

Lark froze. "Burned?" She described Spinner's son to Mouse and he nodded. She turned to Raven. "It's the peasants they arrested at the service. They are still holding my friends, Raven. Why are they making them attend Fawn's funeral?"

Raven looked at her with pity. "I doubt they're 'attending', Lark."

"It can't be," she said. Lark felt the sickness in her stomach at the thought of her friends buried alive to serve a ritual they no longer believed in. "No. Willow wouldn't entomb them with Fawn."

"They have done it before, my dear."

She brushed the horror aside and took Raven by the arm. First things first: they had to get the prince to safety, now.

"Enough talking," Ox said firmly. "Let's go."

Raven didn't move. "They will kill them like they killed your family, Ox," Raven said, and Lark suddenly realized what Oxen had lost all those years ago. His own family killed, and Raven unable to save them? The old man's bitterness made sense now.

"It doesn't matter," Ox said. "We can't stop them. Nothing matters but saving you, my boy. It's our chance to get out of here and get you home."

He went first, out the door, and they followed into the dark hall. Ox started to lead them further back into the prison halls.

Raven stopped. "Come on," Lark said, urging him on. "Ox is right. You must get out before anyone comes this way."

"That is the wrong direction, my dear," Raven said. "I'm not going that way."

Lark froze.

Ox turned back and took Raven by the arm, trying to push him along. "My Lord, I've been lurking in the catacombs for nigh-on a week waiting for a chance to get to you. You think I don't know the way out?"

Raven stood his ground. "We are not leaving."

He turned to Lark.

"No," she said, shaking her head. "Absolutely not, Your Grace. I will come back for my friends later. You cannot go in there."

"You'll face them alone?" he said. "You against the entire Ariane sisterhood is not what I have in mind for you, my dear." Lark felt a thrill down her spine every time he called her his dear, but this was hardly the time to pause and enjoy the sensation.

Then he raised an eyebrow and smiled at her. "And are you giving me an order, Ariane? I didn't think you were allowed to do that."

"I have been doing a number of things I am not allowed to do, Your Grace. But you cannot risk your life to save my friends. That is something I will not allow."

"I'm sorry, my little Ariane. But you cannot protect me from this. They are not just your friends, they are my people. They are my responsibility. And I will never have a better opportunity to confront Willow."

"Confront her?" Ox sputtered. "Are you daft, My Lord? Begging your pardon, Sir, but—"

Raven smiled. "I am daft. And I am not leaving."

"You are not staying, My Lord," Ox said firmly.

"Relax, Ox," Raven said. "Willow is Ariane. She cannot kill me."

Ox did not smile. "She can. She already did."

Raven quickly looked around. "Come here." He stalked back to the prison cell with them following. After they were all inside, Lark pulled the door almost shut behind them. They were in dimness again.

Raven turned to Oxen. "Explain yourself."

Oxen looked at the ground. "What do I need to explain? You were injured. You were just a boy, a child." His voice broke. "Like my own would have become if he lived. Your eye was useless, your leg almost useless. What else could I do, My Prince?"

"You rescued me. I remember you dragging me away from the fire. But how are you so sure Willow will kill me now? She is Ariane. She fought the peasant murderers—"

Ox shook his head. "No, Your Grace." Oxen walked over to the wall and then stood facing it, as if he couldn't stand to look at them —or couldn't stand to have them look at him. He spoke softly, to the obsidian wall. "I was out by the swan's lake, far from the castle. I was—well, Your Grace, you know I was not myself after my—after your mother was entombed. I was—thinking. The lake was quiet, and it seemed a good place to end it all, deep and still and peaceful. And then I heard voices. It was His Grace, Prince Kestrel, and he was trying to carry you, but he was not that much bigger than you, and he was sick, vomiting and almost unconscious himself. You were bleeding, and lay very still. You were both covered in blood."

"I remember that," Raven said. "But I remember the Ariane were there, guarding us."

Oxen shook his head, then continued his quiet story in that almost emotionless voice, his head down as if he wanted to hide from his own words. "I almost stepped out from behind the ferns. I almost did, and that would have been the end of the story, but then —" He paused. "Then I saw them. It was Autumn and Willow. They came running. I thought—" he laughed, a bitter, ugly laugh. "I thought they were coming to help you. I don't know why I ducked down. If I hadn't...."

"Oh my God," Lark whispered.

"They stabbed your brother, over and over. I hid there and saw it, was sure you were both dead. Then they dragged you back to the castle. I followed, because—" another pause, longer than the previous one, and his voice dropped almost to a whisper. "I thought I saw your hand move as they lifted you, my boy."

Ox shook his head. "There were never any peasant murderers," he said flatly. "It was them. All along, it was them."

"But," Lark cut in. "Almost all the other Ariane died fighting the peasants—no," as she realized what he was saying. "How could

Willow? She would have no reason."

"Didn't she?" Raven asked. "You don't know how things were back then—and what her position was. She is now the leader of the Ariane. She has power and wealth—and, yes, now I see. You say Kestrel was sick when he tried to escape?"

"Yes, Your Grace," Oxen said, still facing the wall. "It was poison. In the tea, perhaps. When the family was unconscious, they went for the servants—they used the chaos to attack. They probably drugged the Ariane, too. Willow must have planned it all."

"But why?" Mouse asked.

"She could see what was coming," Raven said. "My father had overstepped all bounds of rationality. Things could not continue. Kestrel she might be able to manage—but if the people kept pushing for me to be king...."

"She would lose everything," Lark said. "Now she not only leads the kingdom, she is wealthy beyond all measure—of course. All the wonderful riches she possesses. The pearls," she said to herself. Raven looked at her, but she shook her head. "It doesn't matter. She rewarded me for finding you with bloody jewels bought with stolen goods. She must be working with the smugglers—not fighting them. She must have been all along. And her lover, Wolf—"

Raven nodded. "I have been thinking about your description of him. I know who he is. A poor silkworker had been caught smuggling and was sent to the Ariane prison back then. He was in this very cell, I believe. Somehow," he said sarcastically, "his Ariane guard mistakenly allowed him to escape."

"Willow?"

"She was on limited duty and had been reduced in rank for her mistake. She was very angry at her loss of status."

"They are lovers," Lark said with shame. "They have been for years. We do not speak of it, but she broke her vows of chastity a long time ago. Every one of us knows it."

"Perhaps the vow of chastity was made to be broken," Raven said softly.

Lark looked down at her feet. "But it still makes no sense. She would never burn the dead," Lark said. "That is too monstrous to imagine. Only someone sick and evil could do such a thing, no matter what their faith."

"Wolf probably did it," Raven said. "He's a peasant, he doesn't believe in the nobles' gods anyway—"

"He probably doesn't believe in anything, but to do something so horrid, it's inhuman, it's—"

"I did it!" Ox shouted, finally facing Raven. "I did it. Oh my god, don't you understand? I had to save you. Can't you see that? That was all that mattered. You were all that was left. You alone lived. You were the only one who even cared about the people buried in the tomb. Willow would come back. She would count the bodies, she would see you were gone. I couldn't let her find you. I had to do it." He put his head in his hands and his shoulders shook as he sobbed.

Raven put a hand on his shoulder. "Oh, Ox. You could have told me."

He shook his head. "No. If I told you, what would you have done?"

Raven almost smiled. "I would have come marching back into Chÿar with a sword in my hand to smoke the witch out of her lair."

"And gotten yourself killed. You were just a boy. I couldn't let her find out you were alive, Your Grace. She could never know you lived."

"She always knew," Lark said softly. She told them her own memory of that day:

Lark saw in her mind the image of a charred hand. A ring of star sapphire and gold, melting into a dead finger. She dropped the pitcher of water she had been carrying, and the water splashed across the floor.

Then a young Willow was standing over her, saying, "the royal family is dead. All of them. The Griffon line is ended." Willow's silver cloak shimmered in the candlelight as she raised her sword high over Lark's tiny figure.

"But the prince escaped!" Lark said, too stunned to notice the sword. "Prince Raven still lives."

The sword wavered. "Where did the prince go?"

"I saw him go that way." She waved her small hand toward the city gates. "He will be far away by now. But you can go and rescue him."

Willow bent over her. "You saw this? You are sure, little girl?"

Lark nodded. "I thought 'why is the prince limping?' but I had to get the water for more tea, and I knew I would be punished if I didn't hurry." She looked trustingly up at the young woman in the silver cloak. The Ariane warrior would fix it.

Willow towered over her, her eyes on Lark's as if staring into her soul. "He got away. Only an Ariane could track him now," she muttered. She lowered the sword to her side. "What is your name?"

"I am called Lark, Mistress."

"Listen carefully, Lark. The peasant rebels killed the royal family, and most of the Ariane. Without a king, the Ariane must rule until the prince can be found."

The Lady looked down at Lark, her expression stern. "Lark, are you ready to serve your people?"

Lark nodded. "I will do anything you want me to, My Lady...."

"Oh my God, Raven," Lark finished telling the story. "She used me to destroy you."

"No, dear, no."

"Yes, she did. That's why she made me Ariane. I never knew why. I thought"—her voice broke—"I thought she loved me as a daughter. But everything in my life has been a lie. She wanted this. She planned this for fifteen years. She made me the perfect assassin, then sent me to hunt you."

He shook his head.

"Yes. She wasn't sure, maybe, that you were alive. But she wasn't going to take the chance. If there was any possibility that you were out there, and that you knew the truth about her, you were a threat. You could come back and take the power away from her—and worse, you could expose her as the murderer she is."

Raven smiled. "Then that's what we'll do."

Both Ox and Lark shook their heads. "No, Your Grace."

"Yes," he said. "Don't you see? This changes nothing. She is a murderer, and she is destroying this country. People will die to further her plots—they already have died. I alone can stop it."

"She has already labeled you a traitor, a hired killer sent to destroy her."

"Someone there will recognize me. Someone must believe me. All it takes is one, and we have her."

"You can't count on that," Ox said. "It has been fifteen years—no one might know you. The risk is too great. I won't allow it."

"No, really, Raven—Your Grace," Lark agreed. "I cannot allow it. I cannot. It is my mission in life to protect you, and I cannot let you go in there." She turned to Oxen and Mouse. "We will get the prince out of the city before the service ends. I can get us past the gate guards—they won't know we've escaped until it's too late to find us. We will disappear somewhere in the countryside and be free of all this, forever." She turned to Raven. "I'm sorry, My Prince. But it must be this way. We cannot let you die."

He hesitated, then nodded. "I understand." He stepped closer, and dropped his voice to a murmur. "I do understand, my dear." He bent his head to her. "You are my protector, and you can do nothing else. It is who you are."

His lips brushed hers, and she shuddered, as much from the memory of the night they'd spent as from the physical sensation itself. She was shocked he dared kiss her in front of the others, but then forgot all about them in the glory of the touch and taste of him.

He pulled back and sighed.

She looked up at him, feeling such a surge of love and pride she felt she would burst.

"Lark?"

"Hmmm?" she said, still lost in the taste of him.

"I'm so sorry, my dear," he murmured.

"Sorry?" she asked, trying to focus.

Then she saw his fist coming at her, and she was out.

Lark felt herself drowning.

She sputtered up to awareness, a horrible headache following her back to consciousness.

She was soaking wet, her silk clothing a clammy layer clinging to her skin. Ox and Mouse stood over her, an empty bucket in Ox's hand. "Here, boy," he said, handing the bucket off to Mouse, and then he helped her to her feet. "That worked, finally," he said to her. "Wasn't sure if you were ever going to come around."

"He hit you," Mouse said, incredulous.

"He certainly did," she said, rubbing her ear where his fist had expertly landed.

"He never hit me—ever," Mouse said. "Why was he mad at you?"

"He wasn't mad at me, Mouse." Water dripped into her eyes. She shook her head to clear it, then found herself immediately regretting it. "Where is he?"

"You have to ask?" Ox said.

"How could you let him go?!" She took a step forward, then felt dizzy and had to stop. Ox gripped her by one arm, propping her up. "Are you out of your mind, Ox? Oh, God...."

He patiently held her while she vomited. "My boy has a mind of his own," he muttered with grudging respect. "We should have known he wouldn't take orders from us."

When she finished he handed her his own heavy cloak to wipe herself off with. "I won't be needing it where we're going," he said.

"And where's that?"

"He ordered me to take you and the child and escape."

"You idiot," she said. "You were going to do that?"

"Of course not. Been waiting for you to wake up. Took long enough."

Lark gathered her cloak and scabbard and straightened up. She felt better after the sickness: purged, light, ready to face what was coming.

She led the way into the hall. Ox and Mouse followed. "Down to the right and then third opening on the left," she said to Ox and

Mouse. "You can't get past the gate guards, but if you are clever, you can make your way down into the city. Bless you." She kissed Mouse on his forehead.

"How long has it been?" she asked Ox.

"It seemed an eternity—but moments, only."

"I may be too late. He's unarmed."

"He took my knife with him."

"That's not enough to defend yourself against—"

"—a nest of Ariane. Yes. That's why we needed to wait for you."

"We?"

Ox pulled out his cleaver from the thong at his belt. "Yes, Ariane."

They ran.

XVII

The Temple was full.

Lark stood hidden by the entrance with Oxen and Mouse behind her. In the temple she could see not only the rows of nobles standing in their honored places, but in the back of the room, the rows of peasants watching. She could not count how many were there, for they were mostly hidden behind an intricate metalwork screen—so that their poverty would not mar the perfection of the service. There were many, though, which was odd, as peasants did not generally attend these services unless threatened.

The nobles filled the room, standing strictly by rank in marked places they had inherited from their ancestors.

The lowest nobles wore raw unpolished silk in solid colors. The higher the ranking, the more subtle the color combinations, with a sheer pale color over a richer underlayer making shimmering shades that changed as the light passed over them.

Only court-ranked nobles of the eighty leading families could wear patterns: sapphire moths or creamy swans or a forest of emerald trees, each unique, each more beautiful than the last. Lark remembered when she was little seeing the ladies of the court all in their formal gowns, like a field of flowers: wisteria, roses and chrysanthemums. And then the queen, Lady Melody, entered wearing a gown of palest pink covered in a flock of tiny golden birds that flew about her as she moved.

Now the queen's only surviving son stood at the center of the room, leaning on a makeshift cane, dressed in ragged peasant garb, alone against the world.

At front and center in the temple lay a black circle. All the floor was white marble, except the circle the length of five men, made of flawless obsidian, and studded with a pattern of the most precious jewels. A griffon, half lion and half eagle, shone amidst the blackness. Sapphires, gold, diamonds, pearls, every kind of precious stone had been embedded in the circle to make up the symbol of the royal family. Surrounding the griffon were forty-four silver moths made of precious Ariane metal.

The air was filled with the rich honey scent of incense, and in the pure white light of the candles all was color and beauty.

The forty-four Ariane sisters should be standing on their silver moths, by rank, so the ceremony of honoring Fawn could begin.

But where the Ariane should stand was a cluster of confused sisters, looking frightened. Everything in the room was still. Only the hiss of a candle sputtering out could be heard in the deafening silence as all stared at the intruder.

Willow had been seated on the royal throne at the head of the Temple. Now she stood, an impassive judge in shimmering white. Lark noticed her sword sheathed in its jewel-studded scabbard at her side. Unusual that she wore a sword for the funeral service, but perhaps Willow had some sense of what was to come.

Raven stood alone in the center of the circle, on the griffon.

Lark motioned for Oxen and Mouse to stay back. She entered the room and walked to join Raven in the circle.

He said nothing, did not even seem surprised, but merely resigned. They were bound together in this to the end.

Raven touched Lark's arm. She looked where he indicated. Spinner and his son, and the rest of the peasant worshippers arrested last week, were in chains in an alcove behind the grand sarcophagus. It was as Raven said. Willow was planning to kill them all. But now Lark knew the true reason—not because of some religious fervor, or fear of treason, but because Lark might have told them about Raven. So they must die. As Fawn had to die.

Raven's expression grew hard, harder than Lark had ever seen, and she suddenly realized he was not just the sweet boy prince she remembered, he was a judge, and a king.

Willow finally spoke, looking not at Lark but at Raven. "You dare to enter here?"

"I have the right," Raven said. There was muttering among the nobles. No one had the right to step into the circle except the Ariane —and the royal family.

Willow turned to the Ariane and they looked to her, confused. She motioned to Lotus, who took two steps forward.

Lark drew her sword, and Lotus paused.

But then Raven spoke. "Listen to them." He directed this at Lotus, not Willow, and Lotus's eyes grew wide as she listened.

The voices in the crowd of peasants were growing louder. "It is him." "He has returned from the dead." "Prince Raven lives."

The nobles turned to look at the peasants, then looked—really looked—at the man in the circle. They, too, began to murmur among themselves. Raven raised his hand, and a hush fell.

Lotus sheathed her sword and stepped back among the group of Ariane.

Raven said nothing more. He simply stood on the griffon crest and watched Willow coldly, calmly, with that executioner's look in his eye.

"No!" Willow took a step backward, toward her throne. She was like a cat cornered.

"You heard them," Lark said. "You expect us to deny what we see with our own eyes? You must acknowledge him now, My Lady."

"I will not step aside for that stupid boy," she hissed.

"I am not a boy." He said it softly, but all strained to listen. "I am a man, and I am the rightful ruler of the Silver Isle. You live to serve me."

"Why should we believe you? You could be any man. This—" her hand waved at Lark with contempt—"this slave calls you prince and we should accept this? Never."

"It is the truth," Lark said calmly. *Patience,* she reminded herself. *Do not be goaded into losing your temper. If you have learned anything by now, it must be patience.*

"Who are you to say this to me? Why should anyone listen to you? A foundling. A slave I plucked from ruin. I gave you a life, Lark."

"You gave me a life. You did not kill me like you killed all the others." Lark ignored the gasps of shock in the crowd. She turned to face her fellow Ariane. "I saw no peasant murderers that day. I saw Willow, standing over the bodies of the royal household and their loyal guards."

She turned toward the shadowy peasants behind their screen.

"The prince spoke the truth fifteen years ago, that the leader of the Silver Isle was called to lead his people out of darkness, that he was a shepherd over *all* his people, not just the mighty. That the children who burned their hands in the silk cauldrons were as worthy of food and warmth and life as the children of the mighty."

A roar went up behind the screen. They stomped their feet on the floor and called out, "Raven yr Griffon!"

Willow had lost them.

But the nobles in their rows muttered, not so cheerful at hearing the young prince's words.

Raven finally spoke. "But you, Willow, betrayed not only the poor when you murdered my family, but the rich. Whose daughters were slaughtered that day in your quest for power over the Ariane? Their daughters." He pointed to the nobles, and the shifting ceased. Nearly every family there had given a child to the Ariane in the last generation.

"Do you know how these nobles feel about the Ariane now? They clutch their tiny daughters to them, and cry in fear when an Ariane comes to their door. What happened to the nobility of the Order of Silver?"

The Ariane now looked at Willow warily.

"What happened to the honor of those of us born to power? We were not placed on this Isle to sit in our silken chambers and eat sweetmeats and plot against our kin. We are here to bring honor to our land, to our families, and to all of our people. Are we frightened, greedy children to fight amongst ourselves while the Var sit just offshore, awaiting their chance to destroy us? The people of the Silver Isle are a great people. They—we—are better than this."

At last. There he was. The boy Lark remembered: dashing and brave, willing to stand against a thousand if he believed it was right, willing to speak the truth when no one else would.

"The king—my father—betrayed the trust of our people," he continued. "But the people of the Silver Isle did not kill him. A despot did, in a bid for selfish power and glory.

"Is that not what you want?" Willow snarled. "Power and glory for yourself?"

"Has he ever?" shouted someone behind the screen.

Raven turned his back on Willow and faced the room. "She tried to destroy the future of the Silver Isle. She tried to destroy us. Will we let her succeed? I say no. What do you say?"

The peasants shouted again, and this time, the nobles joined them.

Willow looked stunned. "I will not hand over power to a cripple."

"Who made him a cripple?" cried a voice in the crowd of nobles. Lark saw that it was Reed yr Täryn. "Who took our sisters from us to fulfill her own selfish desires? I charge you, Willow y Ariane. I charge you with murder!"

"As do I." Raven said, coldly. "I charge you with treason against the Griffon line. I charge you with treason against your Sister Ariane. And I charge you with treason against all the people of the Silver Isle. You will answer to these charges, Ariane."

"Here in this holy place?"

"What better place to avenge the murder of Fawn y Ariane!" cried Reed.

Lark looked at Reed and then nodded. "Yes. You sent Fawn y Ariane to her death because you feared I would tell her the truth about Prince Raven."

"I sent her to fight honorably to redeem herself," Willow said. "You had corrupted her! She worshipped the peasant god because I allowed a slave to infect our sisterhood with low-caste ideas. You infected her. You ruined her for your own scheming purposes."

"She was my friend," Lark said simply, refusing to be goaded.

Reed spoke again. "She was Fawn's friend. And you sent my sister to her death because you feared what she could do if she learned the truth. I have charged you with murder, Willow y Ariane. Will you answer the charge?"

"She will answer," Raven said quietly. He turned to lark. He said nothing more, but she suddenly realized what he expected of her.

She stepped closer to him and whispered. "My prince. I cannot. You cannot ask this of me. She was mother to me."

That hard look never wavered. "Are you slave or Ariane, Lark? Do you serve me or them?" He nodded to the chained peasants. Then his look softened, and he gently touched her arm. "I'm sorry, my dear. But we each have our roles to play in this."

Lark stepped back from him.

This was it. He was right. She must decide once and for all who she was. Was she of the lowest caste?—then she must fight to protect her people. Was she of the highest caste?—then she must uphold the law. Either way she was doomed to face this.

She bowed to him formally. "Yes, My Prince."

The Ariane sisters moved away from Willow's throne.

Lark raised her free hand, setting her cloak glittering again in the reflected glow of the candles. "The prince demands you answer these charges, Willow."

Willow's eyes narrowed as she noticed the change in address.

"I do not accept the charges."

Lark shrugged. "It does not matter whether you accept them. This sin of murdering a sister is unforgiveable and must be paid for."

"Sin?" Willow sneered. "We are not slaves to be bound by the good and evil of the peasant god."

"You prefer the word treason to sin? All right. You are Ariane, bound by the oaths we all took as small children. Our loyalty is to Griffon, Sister, and our People. You have betrayed all three. I charge that you murdered all but one of the Griffon line. I charge that you killed your Ariane sisters"—Lark's voice cracked there, but she continued—"and you have betrayed all of your people with your greed. I charge that you consort with smugglers and steal the wealth that rightly belongs to the people of the Silver Isle." Lark raised her sword.

But Willow did not draw her sword. Instead she held out her hand. "Turn away from this folly, and all will be forgiven, my child. You are one of a kind, little Lark."

The term of endearment brought a tear to Lark's eyes. She blinked the tear away. How could Willow still have such power over her, even now?

Willow saw Lark blink, and pressed the point home. "You are not one of these—" she paused, and then sneered, "—peasants." Again the hand of the Ariane leader reached out to her. "My child, my dear child. I have raised you up beyond your station. No one has ever done what you have. Will you throw all that away? Are you really so base, so low that you would choose them over your Sisters? Over the Book of Rule? Over all this?" The wave of her samite-clad arms took in the glowing temple around them, the shimmering jewels on the walls, the silk-clad sisters standing silent in a ring behind Willow, the richly garbed nobles in their ancestral places around the center.

The star sapphires on Willow's throne—the king's throne—winked in the spermaceti candlelight.

Lark wavered. Who was she, a base peasant of the lowest class, to destroy all this majestic tradition?

Willow smiled. That magnanimous, brilliant smile that had captivated Lark as a child. She had won.

Lark took a step toward Willow, and the Ariane guards circled around her.

The room was silent, the stillness tense as a bowstring.

"I forgive you, my child." Willow came forward to take her into her embrace.

At the same time the Ariane guards moved in on Raven, cutting Lark off from him.

"No." Lark's voice was not loud, but everyone froze as if she had shouted.

"I am your leader," Willow said.

"No." Lark shook her head. "I do not serve you, My Lady. I serve the Prince of the Silver Isle."

"I took you from nothing and made you what you are."

Lark shook her head. "No. I made myself what I am. And what am I? Better than these people?" The wave of her arm took in the cluster of frightened peasants chained by the wall. "As you are better than them?"

"You do not have the right to judge me."

"Yes, I do, Willow. Any Ariane has the right to question your decisions."

The other Ariane gasped as they realized the implication of her statement.

Willow looked flabbergasted. "You cannot think that you—a slave—"

"—No longer a slave, Willow. You raised me up to be your sister in arms. To be your perfect assassin. Now you will see the error of doing that. For committing the crimes of murder and treason against the royal family of the Silver Isle you must die." As Lark said the words she realized they were true. Willow must die.

And Lark was the only one who could kill her.

The look in Willow's eyes showed that she knew it, too. Suddenly all protest stopped, from Willow, from the sister Ariane gathered around, and even from the peasants in their alcove.

"Clear the circle," Raven said, and all rushed to obey.

The Ariane left the circle and moved back behind the throne. Raven nodded to her and turned to leave the circle. Ox and Mouse came forward and stood near him just outside the circle.

Lark took a step back into the center of the circle, sword at the ready, her cloak a swirl around her.

"I will not abdicate," Willow muttered.

"You are not being asked to abdicate." Lark raised her sword. "I can and do expect you to defend your position against this challenge." She held her sword in front of her, and spoke the words: "I, Lark y Ariane, out of desire to strengthen the sisterhood of the Ariane and with no thought for personal gain, do hereby challenge you, Willow y Ariane, for your position in the sisterhood." Lark took off her brooch, marked with the hard-earned six, and tossed it in the circle. It skittered across the diamond-studded griffon to rest at the feet of Willow's chair. "I swear to uphold the Rule with my life unto my death. Be at arms, Sister."

Lark took the first stance.

"You cannot."

"Take the position, Willow."

"You must challenge in order. Not six to one. You must challenge in order. You must fight Lotus first. She is next in line before me."

"It is not in the Rule. The Rule says I may challenge who I wish."

"Lotus?" Willow turned to the other woman. Lotus stood rooted, in shock from the look on her face.

Lark looked at Lotus. "Is that not the Rule, Sister?"

Lotus shook herself free from the shock. "Yes...," she said hesitantly. "It is the Rule." She turned to Willow. "My Lady, you know it is the Rule. Lark has the right to challenge you."

"No! It is not right. I will not defend myself against a slave. I am the leader of the Ariane. I do not answer to anyone."

"You answer to me." Raven's voice was soft but clear, and the simple statement silenced everyone. "You will answer to me for your actions, Willow. Here, or with the executioner's stroke. You choose."

Willow finally drew her sword and stepped into the circle.

Lark prepared herself.

"You cannot do this," Willow hissed. "You are not good enough."

Lark felt that familiar ache in her stomach. She was nothing. She was only a slave. Then it finally struck her. "Yes, Willow. I am only a servant of the king of the Silver Isle."

For the first time Willow looked truly frightened. "You are nothing," she said desperately.

Lark thought of Lotus's taunts. "It is a lesson I won't forget," she had told little Fawn. She smiled at Willow. Lesson learned.

She made the first move toward Willow, sounding her out. The Forms were simple, clean. Lark's movement was clear and unhurried.

Willow flailed desperately at the empty air, but Lark was no longer there. She was behind her.

She could kill her from behind, but no. There was more at stake than survival now. At first all that had mattered was keeping Raven alive. But he had been right. Their lives were not the point. This was about truth and honor.

She allowed Willow to turn and face her. Calmness washed over her like a cool waterfall, rinsing her clear of fear and even of hatred toward the murderer who stood before her.

She was Ariane. She would protect the king.

They moved in the patterns Lark had practiced all her life. She quickly saw that Willow had not practiced enough. Lark was always outside Willow's range, dancing smoothly around her.

She saw Willow knew it, too. Willow moved toward her, and Lark prepared for the final attack.

But Willow swiftly leaped over Lark. Lark saw it in slow motion —Willow could not defeat her, but she could finish the crime she had started fifteen years earlier.

Willow's sword stretched out toward the prince. He lunged away, toward the center of the circle, and began to raise Oxen's short knife in defense, but it would not be enough against the Ariane sword.

But Lark's own sword was already there. It sliced cleanly, weight and counterweight in harmony, and Willow's head was severed from her body.

Silence. Utter silence in the temple for ten beats of Lark's heart.

Then, "it is finished," Raven said. The rightful king of the Silver Isle stood on the jeweled griffon in the center of the circle, covered in Willow's blood.

Lark knelt down next to the body, beyond hate or even grief.

"She shall burn," Reed yr Taryn said from just outside the circle, staring with pure hatred at what remained of the Ariane leader.

"No," said Raven quietly. "She will go to her gods as she wished. We were a civilized people once. We will not compound the sins of our fathers."

Raven turned his back on the body, but at that moment, someone lunged at him from the crowd.

Lark scrambled to her feet, but it was too late.

Wolf fell to the floor, clutching at his shoulder where Oxen's short knife protruded.

Raven wiped his hands on his tunic. "This will be her pet smuggler, I assume?"

Lotus pulled the short knife from Wolf's shoulder as he screamed. She wiped it on his cloak and handed it back to Raven. "Shall I kill him for you, My Prince?"

Raven turned to Lark. "Ask the leader of the Ariane guard."

Lark felt the shaking in her body ease as her breathing began to return to normal. Her hands felt slippery and she rubbed them against her cloak lining, leaving streaks of blood on the silver-gray mantle.

"No matter," Raven said softly, so only she could hear. "You will need a new white one, anyway." He raised his voice so all in the room could hear. "Lark y Ariane now leads our personal guard, and we trust her in all matters regarding our safety."

Lotus still stood over Wolf. She swallowed hard, and for a moment Lark thought she might object, but then she simply said, "What is your wish, My Lady?"

"Put him in the prison," Lark said. "I know there is an empty cell."

Lotus dragged the man to his feet.

"And Lotus," Lark added. "Make sure this time he does not escape."

XVIII

Oxen was standing with little Mouse in the queen's ruined garden when Raven approached them. The brilliant morning sun made even the wreck of the garden beautiful, and far off Raven could hear the music already echoing from the castle where the people were gathering for the coronation. Mouse was skipping about, joyous in his new indigo velvet tunic marked with the silver griffon of the king's personal staff, but Oxen looked awkward and uncomfortable in his own fancy new clothing.

Raven noticed for the first time how bent Oxen was. The years had weighed heavily on him.

Oxen sent Mouse scampering off on some errand with a handful of flowers. Mouse waved cheerfully at Raven as he ran off.

Oxen spotted Raven and they walked toward each other until they met amidst the rampant tangle of Mother's herb patch.

"The gardens are in ruin," Ox said gruffly. "It will take much work to bring them back to something worthy of a king."

"You do not need to work, Ox. You can sit on a silken chaise and eat sweetmeats for the rest of your days. You have earned it."

"No, your grace. I—" he paused. "I need to do this. I need to find my way back, as you have done."

"I am still finding my way, old friend. But I have help."

He saw Lark enter the garden, dressed, as they all were, for the coronation at midday. He watched her as she stood at the entrance, gazing back down toward the city of Chÿar far below them.

He wondered how he could once have feared the turmoil she brought into his life. Without her he never would have found himself. He would have lived forever in hiding, denying who he was and what he was destined to be. She had brought him home, in more than one way.

He smiled as she approached, and his breath caught in his throat as she met his gaze and smiled back. She was his only match, he knew that now. But how would they be able to act on that feeling?

Oxen bowed toward them both, then excused himself and went off.

"Your Grace," she said formally, bowing to him. The heavy white silk of her gown seemed to make her movements even more graceful, with the deliberateness of action the formal garb required adding an almost regal quality to her every step. The Ariane silver mesh cloak, now lined in white brocaded silk, glistened in the morning sun.

She looked nervous. How could he blame her? He was terrified himself. Thousands were gathering in the city, awaiting the appearance of their new king. He had much to live up to—not the least of it, his own reputation.

He took her hand in his and they walked silently together through the weeds.

He had never really been prepared to be king. He was not like his older brother, Kestrel. The crown prince was understandably sought after, and his confident swagger had attracted an endless line of noble women to him. Raven had been only twelve when his family was murdered, but even at that age, he had already experienced the insatiable desire people felt toward him. He had known since early childhood that the people were fascinated by everything about him. They wanted to know the prince's favorite color and his preference in foods. They wanted to know what games he played and when he walked in the garden. Looking back it was understandable. But as a boy he had found people's desire to have a piece of him frightening. He hadn't known how to respond to that longing he saw in the faces around him. They never really saw him as a person at all. Like his father, who portrayed himself as a god come to earth, Raven was also seen as a godlike figure to those around him.

"They are gathering in the castle," she said. "Soon we will have to begin the service." The service. Traditional in most respects, out of deference to the still-nervous nobles, but without the part where all sang blessings to the king for giving them an afterlife. Lark and he had decided it was better to say nothing, rather than make a choice of which god to invoke. Let those in attendance choose what they willed.

"It is not too late to run," she said with a smile. "I would not force you to stay."

"If I promise to let you run away, too?" He smiled also. It was too late for either of them to back out now.

"Lark—I was married once," he suddenly said.

They stopped amid the mint, and the scent wafted up between them.

"I know," she said.

He laughed. "I should have expected that. You are an efficient little spy, aren't you?"

She turned to face him, still holding his hand. "You miss her today," she said. "I understand."

He shook his head. "That's not why I brought it up." He tried to figure out how to explain. "She didn't know me. I loved her, and she did me, in that young, naïve way of love—all passion and excitement. And then grief."

"I know. I'm sorry she died."

"She didn't deserve such a death—no one does. But it wasn't love like... like we have."

She looked at him wide-eyed.

"You are the only one who truly knows me, Lark. You know who I am, what I have been, and yet you still tell me the truth, even — especially—when I don't want to hear it. You are beautiful." He let go of her hand and brushed his palm across her cheek. "But many women are beautiful."

"And you can have any of them," she whispered.

He smiled. "I can have anyone. But I only want you. Don't you see? You are my only match. It was always you, you know."

"My Prince?"

"You believed when no one else did."

"I knew you were alive."

"That's not what I mean. You believed in the Silver Isle. In the power of one person to make a difference. In the worth of the peasants. In all of it. When others were evil, or lost, or just weak, you kept steady. You had faith."

He saw tears in her eyes. "I believed in you, My Prince."

"You believed in who I could be, not who I was, and that made me believe it, too."

His head bent down to hers, and his lips brushed against hers. Just a touch, but it sent him reeling.

"My Prince," she whispered. "If Willow was wrong to break her vows of chastity, then we...."

"Willow was a murderer and a seeker of power."

"She wanted love," Lark said simply.

"That was not her primary sin, Lark."

Lark pulled away from him and turned away. "But it was a sin."

"It was against the Book of Rule," he corrected. "And the Book of Rule was written by people, not God."

He put his hand on her shoulder and turned her to face him again. "The Book of Rule was written by the kings of the Silver Isle and the leaders of the Ariane. It seems to me that the King of the Silver Isle and the Lady of the Ariane may need to make some changes in that Rule."

She still looked unsure. "No," she finally said. "We cannot change the world."

He let her go. "We are the only ones who can. And we have a lifetime to figure it out—together. Let it go for now," he added at her still-doubtful look. "For now we have other concerns."

She smiled. "Like not tripping over our garb?"

He laughed again. "Exactly." He pulled her to him, quickly, and kissed her again, this time long and deep and breathtaking.

Then he drew away and straightened his tunic and held out his hand.

"Will you help me be king, Lark y Ariane?"

Lark held out her hand to him. "We will help each other, My Prince."

They went into the castle to face the people.

Coming Next

The Deeds of the Ariane #4
Kestrel Rising: Raven's Dilemma

Raven is now king, and Lark is leader of the Ariane, but that is not the end of their problems. A battle for power is brewing between the silk-rich nobles of the provinces, and the tradespeople in the city of Chÿar who process the raw silk cocoons into fabric.

But even if Raven can make peace between these factions, the Var raiders will continue to block travel between the island and the silk-hungry Irini trading post across the sea.

Raven is offered a way out–a way that will open up the markets, bring wealth back to the Silver Isle, and will end the conflict with the Var once and for all. But the solution to the Silver Isle's problems will destroy everything Raven and Lark have worked for....

Email barb@barbaracoollee.com if you'd like to be first to know when the next Deeds of the Ariane novella is released.

10% of the earnings from each of Barbara Cool Lee's books is donated to charity. The charity for the *Deeds of the Ariane Novellas* is the Second Harvest Food Bank, http://www.thefoodbank.org. A complete list of charities receiving donations is kept updated at http://www.BarbaraCoolLee.com.